"Nick," Jessica said. "What's the mat—"

Before she could finish her sentence, Nick Fox exploded through the air. In an eye-blurring movement he was karate chopping an object out of a strange woman's hands and catapulting it through the air. In another seamless motion, he imprisoned the woman's arm and pinned it behind her back.

The woman was shrieking out loud in terror just as Jessica cried out, "Celine! What are you doing here?" Jessica couldn't believe her eyes. This was no strange woman, this was Celine Boudreaux, one of the nastiest girls alive.

A shocked Jessica watched Nick stare down at Celine, whose arm he was gripping. His gaze slowly made its way to the flapping notebook on the ground, the object he had slammed out of her hands. He shook his head and gently released Celine's arms.

Celine shook back her mane of honey blond curls and glared at him with tear-filled blue eyes. "You could have killed me, you maniac!" she shrilled in her southern-accented voice. "What on earth's your problem? Are you some kind of a nut?"

Nick stood for a second, apparently unable to utter a sound.

Jessica recovered from her shock long enough to whisper under her breath, "Celine is back. And that means trouble can't be far behind."

SWEET VALLEY UNIVERSITY®

His Secret Past

Written by
Laurie John

Created by
FRANCINE PASCAL

BANTAM BOOKS
NEW YORK · TORONTO · LONDON · SYDNEY · AUCKLAND

HIS SECRET PAST
A BANTAM BOOK : 0 553 50507 6

Originally published in USA by Bantam Books

First publication in Great Britain

PRINTING HISTORY
Bantam edition published 1997

The trademarks "Sweet Valley" and "Sweet Valley University"
are owned by Francine Pascal and are used under license by
Bantam Books and Transworld Publishers Ltd.

Conceived by Francine Pascal

Produced by Daniel Weiss Associates, Inc,
33 West 17th Street, New York, NY 10011

Bantam Books are published by Transworld Publishers Ltd,
61–63 Uxbridge Road, Ealing, London W5 5SA,
in Australia by Transworld Publishers (Australia) Pty Ltd,
15–25 Helles Avenue, Moorebank, NSW 2170,
and in New Zealand by Transworld Publishers (NZ) Ltd,
3 William Pickering Drive, Albany, Auckland.

Printed and bound in Great Britain by
Cox & Wyman Ltd, Reading, Berkshire.

To Jacqueline Marie Campo

Chapter
One

"Excu-use me," Jessica Wakefield said angrily as she stumbled. She was nearly knocked off her feet by two guys in grubby-looking leather jackets and greased-back ponytails. They had just shoved roughly past her, nearly singeing her with their carelessly held cigarettes. The Sweet Valley University student center was packed, but that was no excuse for such rude behavior. "Why don't you watch where you're going!" Jessica snapped as the two pushed on ahead.

The taller one with a mustache stopped in his tracks, turned, and sauntered back toward Jessica. "What's your problem, babe?" He smiled and deliberately dropped a cigarette butt inches from her feet.

His companion with a dragon tattoo on his neck was right behind him. "Yeah, princess—you think you own the whole campus?"

Jessica glared. "If I did, I sure wouldn't let *you* losers in."

1

"Oooh, that hurts," Mustache said, clutching his chest.

"That's cold. You must be an *ice* princess." Tattoo leered at Jessica and faked a shiver.

Jessica lifted her chin and squared her shoulders. She wanted to get as far away from these clowns as possible. "Go waste someone else's time," she said haughtily as she swept past them.

"Don't go away mad," one of them called to her. "We were just getting to know each other!"

Jessica heard them laugh as she sailed down the hall. She deliberately closed her ears to anything else they had to say.

Jerks, she thought fiercely. Jessica scowled as she set her purse down on a nearby empty chair. She carefully checked over her cream-colored suede mini and short-sleeved jacket set for burn marks from the cigarette that loser flicked at her. Luckily her expensive, brand-new outfit and the sea blue silk blouse that matched her eyes so perfectly were unharmed.

Swinging up her purse, Jessica shouldered her way through the crowds swarming through the doors to the job center and the resource office. It was Thursday morning, and the student center was bustling more than usual. Students ambled in every direction, and Jessica had to push her way to reach the end of the hallway where the information bulletin board hung.

Tossing back her long golden hair, she marched toward the gigantic cork board that was covered

2

with thumbtacked index cards and papers. They advertised everything from apartments to sublet to students wanting to share rides cross-country to someone giving away free kittens. People selling, people buying, people broadcasting their needs and talents all used the information board.

"What a mess," Jessica said to no one in particular. "I'll just move this flyer for Karaoke Night. . . . Oops! It fell right in the wastebasket. Looks like there's a space for me now." Jessica giggled. She glanced over her shoulder and saw that no one was watching. Somebody bumped her hard from behind, forcing her to drop her thumbtack. She frowned as she knelt to retrieve it.

There are just too many inconsiderate clods around here, she thought. *Too bad we can't ship them all out to a separate campus—someplace far, far away.* Jessica grinned to herself, picturing it. CRU, or Clods "R" Us, would be the perfect name.

She pushed the tack in firmly and stepped back. Narrowing her eyes, she gave a satisfied nod. Her ad looked good, placed strategically between a card that offered belly-dancing lessons and a fluorescent pink paper that promised free all-you-could-drink beer at an off-campus party.

Jessica gloated. Her advertisement was sure to get lots of attention. Not only was it well written, but it was offering a real bargain too. Who knew she would be so talented at writing ad copy? Maybe she'd finally figured out what her major should be.

3

She reread the card: *One compact color television set, barely used, in mint condition. Asking $100.*

Brilliant—short but brilliant, she congratulated herself. Jessica and her twin sister, Elizabeth, were selling their small used television set in hopes of making some extra cash. Elizabeth wanted to buy a bunch of reference books, while Jessica had her eye on a pair of silver high heels from Eckman's Department Store. Schoolbooks for Elizabeth and sexy shoes for Jessica. Just another example of how two sisters who looked exactly alike were such total opposites in personality.

Of course, Elizabeth also thought it would be good for them *not* to have a TV around to interfere with their studies. Jessica had agreed. She was eager for the money and figured she could always catch her favorite soaps, *All My Love* and *City Heat,* at her sorority house. The Thetas always knew the story lines and kept each other informed on new developments. Elizabeth never had time for soaps or anything fun, for that matter.

Elizabeth and Jessica were both freshmen, but each had a completely different attitude toward school. Elizabeth studied hard and devoted much of her free time to working at the university TV station, WSVU. Jessica considered her social life to be her first priority. Academics just got in the way of having a good time.

And I plan on having plenty of good times once I get those shoes, Jessica thought dreamily. So many parties, so little time. She was just deciding if she should mark up the TV's price when her eye caught movement beside her. For a second she considered stepping away from the stranger who was suddenly gazing at the board next to her. *I just hope it's not another scuzzo ready to burn holes in my clothes,* she thought, darting another glance from under her lashes. Her eyes widened.

This guy definitely was not a scuzzo. The word *gorgeous* didn't even begin to describe him.

The man standing next to her was tall and muscular, with shoulders that went on forever. His thick brown shaggy hair looked as if it hadn't been cut in months, and he needed a shave. But he didn't look remotely like the two lowlifes who'd nearly burned her with their cigarettes. On him the faded jeans and snug black T-shirt looked sexy and not scruffy. It was his face, though, that totally blew her away; his features were ruggedly perfect yet sensitive. He looked a little older, as if he could be an upperclassman.

Jessica was just debating whether she should "accidentally" bump into the hunk when he turned and caught her gaze. She found herself staring into a pair of piercing forest green eyes fringed with unbelievably thick, dark lashes.

The hunk smiled at her, white teeth flashing against his tanned skin. Glancing over her shoulder, he read out loud, "One compact color television set, barely used, in mint condition. Asking $100." His voice was husky and deep and make-your-knees-weak sexy.

Jessica found herself blushing. She had written the ad herself, and Elizabeth claimed it was a bald-faced lie. Their TV set was old and the picture was fuzzy, with horizontal lines popping up from time to time. And it was *tiny*, not compact. But Jessica had been determined to get the money for the silver shoes and had ignored Elizabeth's lecturing. Now she felt foolish.

"Talk about perfect timing," the gorgeous man was saying. "I need a new TV and that's a great price." He squinted at the card. "Hmm, it says to call and ask for J or E." He turned to study Jessica, a smile teasing the corner of his lips. "I'm guessing you're J. I'm Nick Fox, possible customer and buyer of your set." He held out his hand.

Jessica shook his hand, which was warm, dry, and firm in hers. She had used their initials in the ad as a precautionary measure. Both she and Elizabeth had had more than their share of dealing with dangerous males. Elizabeth had almost been killed by the insane William White, and Jessica had been nearly assaulted by creepy James Montgomery. Using their initials had seemed like a good idea.

"I am J." Jessica giggled nervously. "Uh, I mean, I'm Jessica. Jessica Wakefield." Jessica fluttered her lashes. She was glad that she was wearing her mini, which showed off her slender figure and long, shapely legs. "How did you guess that I'm J?" she

6

asked coyly, trying to still her suddenly racing heart. She hoped her hands hadn't been sweaty.

"Oh, I don't know. Not many words in the dictionary begin with the letter *J*." He looked down into her eyes, seemingly oblivious to the river of bodies flowing around them. Someone jostled Jessica, and he reached out to steady her. His grasp on her arm was solid but gentle. "*J* always makes me think of something rare and exotic—like jade or . . . jasmine. *J* seemed to suit you more than *E*."

Jessica felt her face heat up. Did he really think she was rare and exotic? His compliments made her head spin, and listening to his velvety voice made it hard for her to breathe. She licked her lips and tried to appear cool, casual. "I don't know how my sister, Elizabeth, would take that comment," she said archly.

Nick shook his head. "I didn't mean *E* was a bad letter. As a matter of fact—*E* can be beautiful, but just not as unique as *J*."

Jessica was secretly glad. She wanted him to think *she* was special, not her twin. Jessica was jolted back to earth when Nick reached to remove her card.

"Wait," she said. "I have something to confess." She reached out her hand to stop him.

Elizabeth tried not to scream. It was hot and stuffy in the bursar's office. For some reason, despite the mild temperature outside, the furnace in the administration building was working overtime, chugging out puffs of hot, stale air. Taking a deep breath, Elizabeth settled more firmly back into the black vinyl chair, which squeaked every time she moved. She adjusted her ponytail, smoothed her white cotton shirt over her khaki slacks, and tried to compose herself. She was not going to budge from this spot until this was settled, no matter how miserable she was.

Elizabeth was sitting across from Mrs. Rackwood, SVU's chief bursar and most unyielding bureaucrat. The woman was as rigid as petrified wood.

"If you would just read the literature on the Community Center Outreach Program, I'm sure you would agree that they are a worthy organization," Elizabeth said. "If SVU would include them in their internship program, not only could other students get internship credits but the community that the program serves would benefit too. Won't you at least reconsider your decision?" Elizabeth had been talking to her for over a half hour and the bursar had refused to concede an inch.

"I'm sorry, Miss Wakefield." Mrs. Rackwood sounded anything but sorry as she shook her head. "But we simply cannot add your little charity to our list of *approved* internships. It's impossible." Beads of sweat were forming on Mrs. Rackwood's high forehead, and for a second Elizabeth was mesmerized by a drop sliding down to the bridge of her needlelike nose. Elizabeth gave herself a mental kick. Now was not the time to zone out.

"Please at least look at the information I've brought you," Elizabeth begged.

For a full thirty seconds Mrs. Rackwood glanced through the documents Elizabeth had handed her. She peered at Elizabeth from over her thick-rimmed black lenses. "My mind's made up," Mrs. Rackwood said coldly. "Your involvement with the Community Center Outreach Program will not count as a university credit. Nor can we invite them to become an affiliate of SVU, even though I'm sure they're legitimate. Furthermore, despite these glowing testimonials from your supervisor"—Mrs. Rackwood squinted down at the paper and continued in her most pompous voice—"Ann Davies, the university has no impartial means of judging the work you did." She smiled falsely at Elizabeth. "I suggest you simply chalk up your outreach work as a good learning experience and leave it at that."

Outrage swelled inside Elizabeth's chest as she pushed back the tears of frustration squeezing behind her eyelids. She was tempted to pound her fist on Mrs. Rackwood's desk and demand that she open her eyes and ears. That she really listen to her. She'd been telling Mrs. Rackwood that the outreach program was more than eager to cooperate with SVU, but Mrs. Rackwood refused to *hear* her.

Apparently taking her silence as compliance, Mrs. Rackwood continued on. "Now, I don't mean to be abrupt, young lady, but we've spent a good part of my morning going over this again and again, and

9

I'm already behind schedule." Mrs. Rackwood directed a pointed look at her watch and folded her hands, a thin smile on her lips.

Elizabeth fixed her gaze on the mass-produced still life of a fruit bowl that hung behind Mrs. Rackwood's desk. The oil painting perfectly reflected the overall bland stuffiness of the entire room. Looking at the picture helped Elizabeth to keep her temper under control and her facial expression polite. She took a deep breath and kept her voice even.

"Mrs. Rackwood, I understand your position, but the outreach program is worthwhile and valuable. I think SVU would benefit by affiliating itself with them." Elizabeth met the bursar's eyes directly, her voice earnest. "We've reached close to twenty needy families in the area and helped them find resources like decent medical care, nutritional food, affordable day care—all the things they need to better their lives. And we've helped these families in just a few short months. Think what we could do if the program was expanded."

Elizabeth felt herself wilt in defeat as she watched Mrs. Rackwood's stony face, her stiff smile frozen in place. Elizabeth hadn't made a dent. She had been so certain that the university would award her at least two credits for her outreach internship, but Mrs. Rackwood made it clear they weren't going to give her one single credit. It wasn't the denial of the credits that bothered Elizabeth so much as her concern for the program itself. Ann Davies had been so hopeful that the university could open doors for her center. SVU could really help the outreach program and the many families out there who so desperately needed assistance. But Elizabeth had failed. Her arguments hadn't convinced them. SVU wasn't going to give Outreach or Elizabeth Wakefield a chance.

The silence in the office was deafening, and Elizabeth was ready to call it quits when the door suddenly flew open.

The well-dressed, middle-aged man who came charging in stopped dead in his tracks. With an abashed expression he glanced from Elizabeth to Mrs. Rackwood. "I, uh . . . I'm sorry. I didn't know you had company," he stammered. "The girl out front said I should just go right in." He blinked uneasily.

Mrs. Rackwood's tight smile widened a fraction. "That's quite all right. Marlene must be distracted today."

Elizabeth speculated that if the intruder had been another student, Mrs. Rackwood's reaction would have been entirely different. This was a distinguished older man in an expensive-looking suit, and Mrs. Rackwood was forced to be polite.

Mrs. Rackwood inclined her stiffly curled gray head in the man's direction. "How can I help you?"

The man's brown eyes sparked with emotion. He took a nervous step toward Mrs. Rackwood's desk, casting an apologetic smile in Elizabeth's direction. "Mrs. Rackwood," he began, discreetly reading her

11

name plaque on the front of her desk. "I have a very unusual situation, and I need your help. This may sound strange, but I'm searching for my son, whom I've never met." He paused, gulped a breath, and continued. "I know very little about my son except that his twenty-first birthday is sometime this month. I also know his mother's maiden name, which is Antoniani. He may be using that as his last name." The man's voice began to tremble as he laced his hands together. Elizabeth guessed he was trying to keep them from shaking. "If there is anything you can do, any information you can provide . . . I believe my son may be a student on your campus—"

Mrs. Rackwood broke in quickly. "I'm sorry, but I can't help. Our student records are confidential, and there's nothing I personally can do to get around that." The bursar rose from her seat, handed Elizabeth's papers to her, and briskly gathered up her briefcase. "Now, if you two will excuse me." She strode to the door and waited. "I'm late for an important meeting." She tapped her foot meaningfully.

Elizabeth and the man exchanged looks and quickly followed Mrs. Rackwood out of her room and into the main office area. They watched as she swept purposefully through the sliding doors and down the hallway. Elizabeth tapped the man's shoulder. He was standing as if stunned.

"If you want to follow me out to the lobby, we can talk out there. I think I might be able to help you," she said in a gentle voice.

12

Secretaries and student aides pecked away at PCs in surrounding cubicles. Phones rang. The receptionist, Marlene, didn't even glance their way.

He nodded gratefully. "Certainly. If you could help at all, I would be thrilled."

The lobby was nearly deserted. Most students were on their way to lunch, and the staff wouldn't be leaving for their break for another hour. Near a window Elizabeth found two hard-cushioned gray chairs that matched the bleak walls. She motioned the man over. A scarred faux marble table stood between the chairs, and Elizabeth dropped her internship papers on top of it.

"I appreciate your taking an interest—considering I'm a perfect stranger, miss—" the man began.

"Elizabeth," she corrected warmly. "I'm Elizabeth Wakefield."

"George Conroy," he said, holding out his hand.

They shook hands and exchanged pleasant smiles. The old clock on the wall chimed, announcing it was a quarter past the hour.

"Whew." Mr. Conroy shook his head. "Your bursar's not exactly the warm and friendly type, is she?"

"That's an understatement," Elizabeth said wryly. "But *I* do want to help. Not everyone at Sweet Valley University is cold and indifferent, you know." She tapped her finger on her chin and frowned for a second. "I was thinking you might have better luck at the registrar's. They might be able to track down information on your son." Elizabeth frowned and bit

13

her lip. "They go to lunch in about an hour, so you should head over there as soon as possible."

"Thanks. That's a great idea. I just hope it works." Mr. Conroy tried to smile. He ran his hands through his thinning brown hair, looking suddenly weary.

He was an attractive man for his age, Elizabeth thought, tall, stocky. And despite the receding hairline and bags under his eyes, she decided he had a likable face.

"I would do absolutely anything to find my son. He's my number-one priority right now." Mr. Conroy's eyes were deadly earnest as they fastened hopefully onto Elizabeth. "I know it's late in the game to suddenly be playing dad. I know I'm a stranger, but I plan to make it up to him. I just hope . . ." Mr. Conroy's voice trailed off.

Elizabeth felt her heart contract at the look of pain and vulnerability on his face.

Even though he was a virtual stranger, it felt natural to pat his hand. "I don't want to intrude, but I understand how important family is. My loved ones mean everything to me." Elizabeth gave him an understanding look. Elizabeth loved her own family very much. *But there's no bond like the one I share with Jessica. We're more than just twins.*

"Elizabeth," Mr. Conroy asked suddenly. "I don't suppose you know anyone with the last name Antoniani. I could spell it for you—*a-n-t-o-n-i-a-n-i*." He looked both hopeful and doubtful.

14

She shook her head. "I'm sorry. I wish I did. This must be very difficult for you, Mr. Conroy. I wish I could help." She looked up, her eyes lit with sudden inspiration. "Why don't I walk with you? The registrar is in the building next to this one, and I can lead you to the right office."

"I couldn't impose—" he objected halfheartedly.

"Nonsense, I want to help." Elizabeth smiled at him earnestly. "If the registrar doesn't work, we won't give up. I have resources. I'm a reporter at WSVU, and there's bound to be records somewhere about your son if he's here at all." *I'd love to know the whole story behind this man's quest,* Elizabeth thought. *It would make a great human-interest piece.*

A smile trembled on Mr. Conroy's lips, and there were sudden tears in his eyes. "You're a doll, Elizabeth. It must be my lucky day because I've run into you. You've given me hope too. Maybe this isn't as impossible as it seems."

"We'll find your son, Mr. Conroy. I promise," Elizabeth said eagerly. Outside, the sun was shining and the air smelled sweet and fresh. An administrative type in a suit and glasses hurried past them, which reminded Elizabeth that they didn't have much time before the registrar's closed for lunch. As she walked with Mr. Conroy across the sidewalk she scolded herself silently. *Oh, why did I make that promise? What if I fail and break Mr. Conroy's heart? Then I'll feel so bad. Maybe Tom is right—maybe I am too impetuous sometimes.*

15

Elizabeth and her boyfriend, Tom Watts, were both reporters at WSVU, which was where the two of them had first met and fallen in love. Tom was the station manager and Elizabeth's boss, although he only occasionally laid down the law. Sometimes their work relationship did make waves in their personal one, but for the most part the two of them were well matched and happy. They both loved journalism and had been successful at it, uncovering real stories, serious stories with depth. Elizabeth had managed some impressive journalistic victories on her own too, like her story on the gambling-ring scandal involving the athletics department. That had been quite a feather in her cap.

Mr. Conroy's story would be a real heart-warmer, the kind of story that made people laugh and cry. Of course, Mr. Conroy and his son would have to agree to be interviewed and written about. But that wouldn't be too hard—people always loved sharing their happy endings. And a positive story would be a welcome change from all the grim stuff she and Tom had been doing recently.

Elizabeth felt a little tingle of excitement race up her spine, the kind set off by investigative fever. The reality of the registrar's office loomed in front of her, jarring her out of her euphoria. *Before you start congratulating yourself, Elizabeth Wakefield, just remember what you promised this man,* she reminded herself. *Somehow, somewhere, you have to track down his long-lost son.* In the past Elizabeth had dug into much more complex investigations, which had demanded persistence, nerves of steel, and resourcefulness. Finding Mr. Conroy's son had to be easier than her earlier assignments. At least, she reassured herself, she couldn't possibly get into trouble with this one.

She was dead. Alexandra Rollins was in major trouble and she knew it. She trudged across campus to her Western philosophy class, feeling as if she were walking to her execution. The sun beat down on her head and birds sang mercilessly from the trees above. Today was her big exam and she was going to blow it. Her brain had just turned into a sieve, and every little fact she'd crammed into it last night had oozed out.

Alex tugged at her oversized mint green shirt. She had just discovered a silver-dollar-sized splotch of coffee on the front of it. Uneasily she shifted her books to hide the stain. And worse, her new jeans, which had looked so sexy when she'd tried them on in the dressing room, now felt too tight. She didn't have any time to run back to her room and change.

Along with her upcoming exam, Alex was haunted by a twenty-five-page paper due next week in world literature. The professor demanded a typo-free report or points would be taken off. Alex's report was filled with errors, and lately she was all thumbs on the PC. She had revised her assignment three times already.

Alex was also falling behind in economics, and her study group wasn't helping her at all.

Her boyfriend, Noah Pearson, was walking—no, bouncing—beside her, a happy smile on his face. He squeezed her shoulder. "Cheer up, Alex. It will all be over soon."

"I know. My entire college career is about to go up in smoke," Alex muttered.

"Don't be silly. All you need is confidence. You know you'll ace this exam," he said bracingly. Noah's brown hair was still sleek from his shower, and his shirt was neatly pressed. In comparison Alex felt like a slob.

"If you say so." Alex stopped in her tracks. An eyelash had embedded itself in her eye. She tried blinking it out. Her eyes watered, and a tear trickled down her cheek. She pulled a tissue from her purse and dabbed at the mascara running down her face.

"Come on, Alex. You went to all your classes and studied like crazy. You're worrying over nothing." Noah took the tissue from her and wiped gently at her cheek. "You missed a spot," he explained, his eyes warm as they examined her face. He tossed the tissue into a nearby trash can and glanced at his watch. "Uh-oh. My lab starts in ten minutes. Sorry I can't walk you to your Western philosophy class," he said in a brisk voice.

"It doesn't matter," Alex said in a low voice.

Noah apparently didn't hear her. "We'll meet

later for dinner at the snack bar, right?" He gave her a quick kiss and a hug. "Don't obsess about this test. I know you'll do fine." Noah smiled reassuringly as he looked into her eyes. "You're smart and prepared. Remember that." Then he hurried off.

With a heavy heart Alex stood in the middle of the sidewalk and watched him disappear into a stream of people. Noah was a psych major and usually perceptive and sensitive. Lately, though, he had totally misread her moods. He refused to believe that Alex was feeling insecure and tense about school. He kept insisting that she was fine, that she could handle anything. His gung-ho attitude was getting on her nerves.

Noah had been so attentive and ardent before he and Alex became a couple. He'd passionately supported Alex during her struggle with low self-esteem and alcohol. Starting college had been traumatic for Alex, and Noah had helped her through the rough adjustment.

Now Noah acted as if all that was behind her. Just because she was over the hump didn't mean she was fine and dandy. Noah was so nonchalant; he didn't notice that Alex still needed special attention.

Someone suddenly shouted, "Watch out!" A bicycle barreling toward Alex swerved around her just in time.

Alex sighed and stepped out of the way. Maybe she should have let that bike knock her down—then she'd have a legitimate excuse to miss her exam. She peered down at her watch. It was time. She couldn't procrastinate another second. The Western philosophy exam was waiting for her. She had to face this herself. No one could save her now.

"I don't think you want that," Jessica said mournfully.

Nick gave her a surprised look. "Why not? You haven't changed your mind about selling, have you?"

Jessica shook her head, a guilty expression on her face. "No, but this TV's not the bargain I made it out to be." She met his eyes bravely. "Actually it's kind of junky. The picture's not clear and the screen is really, really small." She winced, waiting for Nick's outraged response.

Instead he laughed outright. "Don't look so worried, Jessica. I know the old saying *caveat emptor*— buyer beware. But I appreciate your honesty."

Jessica smiled at him weakly. "I should take the ad down, but Elizabeth really needs the money." Which was only a partial lie, she reassured herself. Jessica crossed her fingers behind her back and lowered her lashes demurely. Maybe Elizabeth didn't need books, but Jessica really needed those silver shoes.

"I still may want to buy your set. Do you have time to show it to me now?"

"Sure. You'd be a lifesaver if you bought it. My sister's pretty desperate, and I really want to help her out." Jessica's face was a picture of selfless innocence,

20

though a twinkle of mischief lurked in her eyes.

Nick looked amused. "Glad to be of service—to you and your sister. Remember, though, I'm only looking. I can't promise I'll buy it."

Jessica nodded agreeably and followed him through the packed hall out into the sunshine. What luck—a major hunk was coming back to her dorm room with her. Now she'd have more time to get to know Nick Fox, and he'd have more time to get to know *her*.

There was something about Nick that reminded her a little of her ex-husband, Mike McAllery. Nick exuded a sense of something wild and free just like Mike had, but luckily Nick seemed more mature. Nick also had a touch of sensitivity that made her think of Louis Miles, a true love from her past who had left Jessica to protect her from his homicidally insane wife. Romantic disasters seemed to trail Jessica no matter how hard she tried to avoid them. Those memories made her excited mood slip a notch.

It was too bright out. Jessica squinted and tugged out a pair of sleek reflector sunglasses from her purse. Slipping them on, she turned to face Nick. "What do you think—could I pass for a Hollywood celebrity, or maybe a spy?"

"Hmm, maybe both. So what are you really?" he teased. "No, let me use my intuition again. I'd guess you're a junior, majoring in international politics."

"International politics!" she squawked, leading

21

him across the sidewalk. "Why, do I look like the scholarly type?"

He shook his head. "No, you just seem like a woman who thinks fast on her feet and who can handle any curveball life throws at her. Perfect traits for a politician."

Jessica tossed her head. "I guess that's a compliment. At least, I'll take it as one. But you're only partially right. I'm a freshman with no declared major, but I am a street-smart kind of woman." She slanted him a mischievous look, a dimple popping up in her left cheek. "And I *definitely* can take care of myself." Her mood was improving by the second.

Without speaking, Nick smiled down at her. They were cutting across the quad, and Jessica noticed how the sun picked out golden highlights in his hair and turned his eyes a brilliant jade. His eyes met hers for a long, fragile moment, and Jessica repressed a shiver of delight.

No, he wasn't really like Mike or Louis. He was totally unique. There was something magical about Nick Fox. He was like quicksilver but also virile and powerful. He was the first guy Jessica couldn't get an immediate handle on. She was pleased that he seemed to be attracted to her and determined to win him over by the time they reached her dorm.

Jessica suddenly noticed that Nick was staring intently up ahead at two girls who were sitting on the grass. The girls weren't unattractive, she decided, watching as one handed the other a soda from a large brown paper bag. But they certainly weren't drop-dead gorgeous. For a long second she was annoyed. People didn't ignore Jessica Wakefield.

"What about you—what's *your* major? Wait—don't tell me," Jessica perkily broke the silence. She pretended to scrutinize him. "I bet you're in psychology. That's why you're so perceptive."

Nick started and seemed to shake himself out of a trance. "I'm sorry, what were you saying?" He threw her an apologetic look. At least he wasn't staring at those other girls anymore.

Jessica pouted. "Weren't you listening? I asked what your major was."

"I'm like you—I haven't declared a major yet," he answered easily.

"OK, maybe I was wrong about your major, but I'm sure I'm right about this—you're new here, aren't you? I know I would have noticed you before." She had a triumphant smile on her face.

"You're right. I recently transferred here." Nick's green eyes flicked over her face.

Jessica shot him a curious look. "Where'd you transfer from, and why SVU? We're not really big or famous or anything."

"Oh, I came from some small college upstate. I'd heard a lot about SVU—that it had an excellent curriculum and an outstanding campus." He grinned carelessly down at her. "Transferring seemed like the thing to do."

"So what was your old college like?"

23

"Ordinary—boring," he said with a shrug.

"What did you say the name was?" Jessica decided to be crafty. She'd get the details one way or the other.

Nick's gaze slid from hers. "I didn't." His heavy lashes obscured his eyes. "Anyway, I'm glad I switched schools."

Jessica noticed again that Nick was checking out the scenery, and not just other girls either. Nick scrutinized each and every person who went by. Jessica wanted those green eyes focused exclusively on her. She never played second fiddle to anybody or anything.

"Well, you must be a junior or a senior. Isn't it hard to move when you're an upperclassman?" Jessica pressed on, fixing a probing gaze on his face.

"I'm a junior. But I didn't mind the change. I like a good challenge now and then."

"I *still* think it's weird that you chose to transfer to Sweet Valley University." Jessica paused, hoping for more details.

Nick shrugged but didn't answer. He walked a little faster.

Jessica sped up too. She studied him closely. "You don't like to talk about yourself, do you?"

Nick looked uncomfortable for a second before smiling quickly. "It's not that. I'm just too boring," he joked. "There's got to be thousands of more interesting things to talk about. For instance, I'd rather hear all about SVU." He slowed his pace and

24

waved his hand around at the surrounding grounds. "Like, where are all the hot spots around here, anyway?"

Jessica preened. "You're in luck. I'm the perfect person for you to talk to. I happen to know where *all* the real action takes place around here." She flipped her hair over her shoulder and shifted her purse. "Starting with my sorority house, Theta house, which is the greatest. My sisters are not only beautiful but fun and cool too." *Not including Alison Quinn, of course,* she added silently. She wrinkled her nose for a second. "Well, most of them are. I guess I'd have to include the Sigmas too. They're a pretty cool fraternity. Most of the guys are decent. I think you'd like them. Both of our houses throw excellent parties." She gave him a quick once-over. "I don't think you'll have any problems meeting people."

"Hey, if you think I'll fit in, I'll take that as a good sign." His glance at her was both admiring and teasing. His husky voice brushed her like fur, sending an electric current through her skin. "Why do I have the feeling that you're a major mover and shaker at SVU?"

"Is that your intuition talking again?" Jessica retorted pertly. "I do have a lot of friends, but I don't think of myself as a major player." She lowered her eyes, a humble expression on her face.

"I think you're being modest, Jessica," he said knowingly. "But I would like to meet your friends."

25

Jessica sparkled up at him. At least he was only looking at her now. "I'd be happy to show you around. The first people I'll introduce you to are my two closest friends, Isabella Ricci and Lila di Mondicci—well, actually she's back to Lila Fowler now." Jessica took a breath to explain. "She was briefly married to an Italian count, but now she's a widow and using her maiden name again." Jessica halted in her tracks. "Oh, look, we're right in front of my dorm. We almost walked right by it."

Nick froze, apparently deaf to Jessica's comments. Jessica was momentarily taken back by the suddenly savage, intent expression on his face. In that same second Jessica caught a glimpse of a woman walking up behind Nick.

"Nick," Jessica said, taking a step toward him. "What's the mat—"

Before she could finish her sentence, Nick exploded through the air. In an eye-blurring movement he was karate chopping an object out of the woman's hands and catapulting it through the air. In another seamless motion he imprisoned the woman's arm and pinned it behind her back. Jessica suddenly realized who the woman was as Nick grabbed her other arm.

The woman was shrieking out loud in terror just as Jessica cried, "Celine! What are you doing here?" Jessica couldn't believe her eyes. This was no strange woman. This was Celine Boudreaux, a fellow student at SVU and one of the nastiest girls alive.

Nick stared down at Celine, whose arms he was gripping. His gaze slowly made its way to the flapping notebook on the ground, the object he had slammed out of her hands. A fourth person's loud gasp made Jessica and Nick turn around. Another girl was standing in the shadow of the trees. Three pairs of wide, shocked eyes swung back around in unison to stare at Nick in disbelief. He shook his head and gently released Celine's arms.

Celine pushed back her mane of honey blond curls and glared at him with tear-filled blue eyes. "You could have killed me, you maniac!" she shrilled in a southern-accented voice. "I just tapped your shoulder with my notebook to get your attention. What on earth's your problem? Are you some kind of a nut?"

Nick stood for a second, apparently unable to utter a sound.

Jessica recovered from her shock long enough to whisper loudly under her breath, "Oh no. Celine is back, and that means trouble can't be far behind!"

Chapter Two

Misery was supposed to love company, but Tom Watts only wanted to be alone. He sat in his sociology class tracing aimless circles on his notepad with his pen. As the circles became a tangle of dark, jagged lines, he realized how much his doodles reflected his present mood.

Professor Kase droned on and on in the background. "In the Jewish tradition," his sociology professor lectured, "a young boy becomes a man when he is bar mitzvahed. At age thirteen his family, friends, and temple congregation help him through this transition with a ceremony."

A man at thirteen years old. Tom was almost twenty-one, a junior at SVU, and sometimes he didn't feel like an adult at all. Like right now, for instance. His birthday was coming up this Saturday, and all he wanted to do was climb in bed, pull the covers over his head, and forget all about it. Birthdays—who needed them?

You used to love them, Tom reminded himself gloomily. *Back when you had a family to celebrate with*. Back before his entire family had died in a horrible car accident, thanks to him. *If they hadn't come to see my football game, they never would have died. If I hadn't been such a hotshot, expecting them to attend my stupid games . . .* The pain welled as fresh and sharp as if the accident had happened yesterday.

Tom closed his eyes and fought back yet another wave of gut-wrenching misery. He massaged his forehead, but the memories still came. A flashback of his own thirteenth birthday materialized. His parents had rented an ice arena, where he and his friends had skated all day. Later his parents had treated all the kids to pizza. After dinner that night it was just family. Everyone sitting around, eating cake, laughing, and opening presents. His mother aiming her camera at him, saying, "Smile, Tom. You're on *Candid Camera!*" just like she always did.

His sister had insisted on helping him open his presents. His brother had made ridiculous faces for the camera, and his father had laughed hysterically. . . .

Professor Kase was rattling on in a slightly louder voice. Tom took a deep breath. He really should be listening to this lecture. It was important. Pen poised, he strained to focus on the professor's monotone.

"Family structures vary from culture to culture. Many are of the patrilineal type. One interesting

29

example is the Kapauka Papuans. In their villages all males are connected via a common ancestor. It's traditional for sons to live with or near their parents, bringing their wives into the household. . . ."

Tom's mind drifted again. The Papuans of New Guinea had nothing to do with his personal situation. And his emotions were so intense at the moment that they drowned out everything but his immediate despair. The agony was relentless, and his imagination refused to show him any mercy.

His family would have loved celebrating his twenty-first birthday with him. His dad would have insisted on making reservations at the finest restaurant, ordering a bottle of wine to honor his becoming an official adult. His mother would have had her camera flashing and probably a camcorder too. She'd urge him to eat a big meal—she was always worried about him getting enough food. There would be cake, chocolate, because that was his sister and brother's favorite, and Tom wasn't that picky himself.

"Mr. Watts, what is your opinion on parallel American traditions?" Professor Kase's voice sang out across the room.

Tom was oblivious. He had been in the middle of imagining his family meeting his girlfriend, Elizabeth, when the professor called out his name. Elizabeth Wakefield was more than Tom's girlfriend; she was also his trusted coworker at WSVU and his soul mate. She not only shared his dreams but his ambitions as well. An image of Elizabeth's delicate, lovely face briefly warmed his heart. She was more than a pretty face, though. She was bright, sensitive, and caring. His parents would have gone crazy over her. She was just the kind of girl they'd hoped he would meet and end up with. And Elizabeth would have loved them too.

"Mr. Watts, if I may have your attention, please." This time Professor Kase's voice, several decibels louder, penetrated Tom's daze.

Tom came back to reality with a thud. "I'm sorry, sir. I wasn't listening."

"That, Mr. Watts, was perfectly obvious," came the professor's sardonic reply. "Now, class, I have some slides to show. If you will direct your attention this way, please. . . ."

Tom groaned softly as the lights dimmed. If today was any indication of how his entry into adulthood was going to turn out, then he might as well skip the whole thing.

The young woman from the registrar's office shook her head sadly as she peered at Elizabeth and Mr. Conroy from over her computer terminal. "I've checked our records, and the name Antoniani just doesn't come up. I've even tried using various spellings." She pushed her glasses back up her nose. "Sometimes people's names are stored under incorrect spellings," she explained. "But nothing remotely like Antoniani has turned up." She looked truly regretful.

Mr. Conroy had told her his story and had apparently touched her heart. She had been searching through SVU's computer files for several minutes.

Elizabeth and Mr. Conroy exchanged disappointed glances.

"Well, at least we know that it *is* possible to access student records and that Mrs. Rackwood was wrong," Elizabeth murmured, trying to be comforting.

Mr. Conroy nodded, staring down at his clenched hands. "You're right. It is encouraging not to get another door slammed in my face."

The young woman suddenly interrupted. "I have an idea," she said eagerly. "We used to list the student's mother's maiden name on his or her records. We have some of that data on microfiche. Let me check with my supervisor to see how recent the microfiche records are." She rose and wound her way back through the cubicles.

Elizabeth watched anxiously as the clerk leaned down to speak intently with an older woman who was sitting in a slightly larger cubicle. The clerk's face told the bad news as she walked back toward Elizabeth and Mr. Conroy.

"I'm sorry, but those records only go up to 1987, way before your son's time, I'm afraid." Eyeing Mr. Conroy's crestfallen face, she added, "Are you sure you have no idea what his first name could be? Because I could do a search using a first name. It might take longer, but still—"

Mr. Conroy shook his head. "I don't have the slightest idea what his first name could be. The one thing I do know is that he wouldn't be named after me," he said, smiling shakily.

His attempt at humor made Elizabeth's heart ache. What a letdown their venture had turned out to be. But they couldn't give up. Elizabeth found herself incredibly motivated, more so than usual. Something about Mr. Conroy struck an emotional chord. She wasn't going to stop—she would find Mr. Conroy's son no matter what she had to do.

Elizabeth smiled warmly at the clerk. "We appreciate everything you've done for us. Not many people are willing to go out of their way to help a stranger."

"You've been very kind. This university is lucky to have someone like you working for them," Mr. Conroy added quickly.

The young woman flushed with pleasure. "Good luck with your search. I hope you find your son."

Elizabeth and Mr. Conroy walked out of the registrar building. The encounter with the registrar's office had been pleasant, if not helpful. But it seemed almost cruel for it to be such a beautiful day, Elizabeth thought. It was as if the sunshine were mocking Mr. Conroy's unhappiness. Elizabeth eyed Mr. Conroy and tucked her internship papers into her purse. While that mission might have failed, she could at any moment be hit by a bolt of inspiration. That was the way a good journalist worked. A reporter dug for the facts and came up with unexpected information along the way, often when she or he was least expecting it.

"Well, Elizabeth, that route didn't pan out, but I'm not quitting," Mr. Conroy announced. "I'm going to check myself into the Sunny Ridge Inn and hang around here until I get some answers. I'm not leaving until I find my son, and that's a promise I've made to myself."

"Good for you. The two of you are destined to find each other. I just know it." Elizabeth caught a glimpse of her watch. She was supposed to meet Tom for lunch after his sociology class. "I just had a thought. You know they always say that two heads are better than one. Well, if you don't think I'm butting in, I'd love to keep on helping you with your search."

Mr. Conroy glowed. A genuine smile lit his face, temporarily erasing the lines of strain. "You are an outstanding young woman, Elizabeth. It's rare to find such a caring person these days, and I gladly accept your offer. I can't tell you how much this means to me."

Elizabeth was almost embarrassed by the depth of his gratitude. After all, she hadn't accomplished a thing for him yet. *Getting father and son together is more important than any story I can write,* she reminded herself sternly. She smiled warmly at him. "Why don't we meet for coffee in the snack bar early tomorrow morning? We can do some serious brainstorming." Elizabeth snapped her fingers. "Oh, wait. You're a stranger on campus, so you probably need directions—"

"That's all right, Elizabeth. I know you must have somewhere else to go. I can always ask for directions if I need to." He patted her hand gently. "I have to thank you again, though. It's unusual to meet such a giving person, considering we're almost strangers."

She shook her head, her blue-green eyes shimmering with emotion. "We're friends by now, Mr. Conroy. I'll meet you tomorrow at eight A.M., and we'll see what we can come up with."

At his nod she waved and hurried across the quad. Tom would be getting out of class any minute. She couldn't wait to see him. *This is what journalism is all about,* she told herself happily. *Writing a story that not only inspires but also shows that love and family can transcend all else.* She knew that Tom would love to hear about Mr. Conroy and his heartfelt quest to locate his son.

This is hopeless. Why don't I just turn the test in completely blank? Alex thought in dismay as her head pounded mercilessly. She stared at the blank paper in front of her and barely heard her Western philosophy professor tell them they had ninety minutes to complete the exam. Ninety minutes. It could have been a thousand, and Alex still wouldn't know the answers.

Her eyes began to blur as she read down the list

of questions. With a dry mouth she realized she didn't remember a single fact from her notes.

The classroom was airless and stuffy, even though it was large enough to seat a hundred people. Only half of the chairs were filled, but Alex felt closed in and trapped. She eyed the exit with longing. It took all her control not to run for the door.

Alex peered under her lashes at the other people in her class. They were all industriously writing, pens moving busily. The professor had insisted that they use only blue ink pens. Alex had written her name, but not a single other stroke.

Panicky tears were starting to build behind her lashes. *I have to at least try to figure out these questions,* she told herself over a thumping heart. Her hands were damp as they tried to grab the pen more securely.

Her eyes slid down the page until they fell on a familiar phrase. Question number thirteen. *Explain in depth the concept of "Occam's razor."* Thirteen was supposed to be unlucky, but a vague memory surfaced in Alex's brain. Occam's razor—it had something to do with mathematics. But what? Alex drew a total blank. She had to write down something, even if it didn't make sense, she decided. *Remember what Noah said, "You're smart and prepared."* Ha. With trembling fingers she began writing.

And then disaster struck—her pen ran out of ink. Alex pounded and shook it, but it was useless. She wanted to scream out loud—why hadn't she brought another pen? Brushing away sweaty wisps of hair from her forehead, Alex snuck a look at the clock. Forty-five minutes had already passed! Adrenaline pumping, Alex dug wildly through her purse but didn't find a single blue ink pen.

It was then that she noticed Tami What's-her-name sitting one seat over. Tami had three pens neatly lined up on her desk, and Alex was desperate. Casting a furtive look in the professor's direction, she whispered, "Tami. My pen doesn't work. Can I borrow one of yours?"

Tami didn't hear her. She was probably too busy sailing through the test with flying colors.

Alex whispered louder, but Tami still didn't hear her. Something made Alex look up. The professor was heading her way. Alex could feel her face burning and her stomach swirling.

The professor was standing in front of her. "Is there a problem, Alexandra?"

Alex gritted her teeth. *Only my whole life,* she thought, disgusted.

Noah might not realize it, but Alex knew she was a mess. How long would it be before she fell apart completely?

Nick cleared his throat. "I'm sorry, really. I totally overreacted. But if you grew up in my neighborhood, you would attack anyone who came up behind you with something in their hand. If you didn't, you could end up with a gun at your head or a knife at your throat." He looked at the three shell-shocked girls who were gaping at him in disbelief. "In my part of L.A., only the quick and the aggressive survive."

Nick knelt down and scooped the notebook up from the sidewalk. He handed it to Celine with a remorseful smile.

Celine grabbed it from him silently.

Unbelievable, Jessica thought. *Too bad Nick didn't slug her one across the chops.* Celine Boudreaux was bad news. Seeing her pop up from out of nowhere was like a nightmare come true.

Jessica grimaced and then started in surprise as the other girl stepped out of the shade. *Oh, great. Alison Quinn—my number-one enemy—is here too.* As if one nightmare wasn't enough. Jessica couldn't believe those two were together, but then, vultures of a feather flocked together.

"What are you doing here, Celine?" Jessica asked sweetly. "I thought you had disappeared from the face of the earth."

Alison Quinn broke in haughtily. "Not that it's any of your business, Jessica, but poor Celine is struggling to get her life back." She linked her arm through Celine's. "And I'm going to help her. This girl has been a victim of circumstances, and she needs the right kind of support to help her recover." Alison looked coldly down her sharp nose at Jessica.

Celine lowered her long lashes. "Alison's been just too kind. I feel like we're almost sisters."

38

Jessica tried not to gag. She caught Nick's eye and threw him a significant look. As perceptive as he was, he'd probably realize that Alison and Celine were poison and that the sooner he and Jessica got rid of them, the better.

Nick's green eyes were bright with interest and some other unreadable expression as he turned to Celine. "I'm just glad I stopped myself in time," he said sincerely. "I would've hated to have really hurt you."

Jessica felt a tingle run up her spine. Too bad Nick did stop himself in time. *If anyone deserves to be roughed up, it's Celine,* she thought. Jessica would love to see Nick in full action someday. She guessed he could be pretty dangerous under the right circumstances. An image of Nick—his tough, fierce side fully unleashed—made her heart accelerate. She just had to get to know him better. If anyone could get under Nick Fox's skin, it was Jessica Wakefield.

Jessica brushed back her hair and tried to will the gruesome twosome away. Unfortunately it didn't work, and there they stood, glued to the sidewalk.

"I hope you'll accept my apology," Nick said, apparently unaware of Jessica's frustration.

If only you'd stop talking to them. Stop being so charming, Nick, Jessica thought. *Then they might fly away on their broomsticks.*

Celine smirked, reading Jessica's irritated face accurately. *Well, well, well, if it isn't Princess Pill's twin sister, and with her nose out of joint too. Just you wait, Miss Jessica. The fun has only begun.*

Celine's outrage was subsiding as she checked her assailant out. Tall, muscular, with a handsome face and a sexy little streak of violence. And as a bonus he had those piercing green eyes. He was just what the doctor ordered. Celine licked her lips. She hadn't seen such a fine specimen of the male animal in a long, long time. His seedy background only spiced up his appeal.

She stepped forward and extended a slender, pale hand. "Apology accepted, but only if you accept mine." She opened her blue eyes wide. "After all, this little accident was partially my fault. I shouldn't have startled you."

Nick shook her hand. "That's very sweet of you to say, but untrue." He grinned down at her.

Celine smiled prettily up at him. "I thought you were Brad Lyons from the Sigmas. Though now that I see you up close, I don't know how I could have made such a mistake. Brad isn't half as good looking as you," she said silkily. "My name is Celine Boudreaux, and I'm so glad we've met, even under such trying circumstances." She flicked her long honey blond curls over her shoulders and took a deep breath, the better to show off her curvaceous shape, perfectly revealed in a clingy powder blue knit dress. She thought she was lucky to have such assets to flaunt.

As Nick told her his name, Celine discreetly nudged Alison with her foot.

Alison darted her a quick look of understanding and stepped forward, clearing her throat. "Jessica, I'm throwing a special formal dinner party tomorrow. It's going to be held at Theta house, and it's going to be *more* than just a party. I'll be making a surprise announcement that affects our entire sorority." She smiled, her pale eyes cold. "Of course, you're invited. I hope you can make it. I promise you won't want to miss this."

Jessica gaped at her, then narrowed her eyes, scrutinizing Alison's face. "I'll think about it, Alison. I'll have to check my calendar." She returned Alison's phony smile, smoothing her suede jacket with elaborate care.

Celine could barely hold back a giggle. Watching poor old Jessica try and figure out Alison's hidden motive was a real hoot. *What was old Granny Boudreaux's saying, "You can lead a horse to water and make him drink, but only if you get him thirsty first"?* And Alison sure was doing a great job of making Jessica thirsty—whetting her curiosity. It didn't hurt for her to see Alison cozying up to Celine either.

"I wish I could make it up to you, ladies. I don't usually start off in a new place by manhandling beautiful women I have yet to meet," Nick said, a teasing glint in his eyes.

Celine sidled closer. "You can make it up to me, Nick," she breathed. "All you have to do is check out my wrist where you grabbed me. It's starting to

hurt. Maybe you can see if it's broken or sprained."
She held out her arm for his inspection.

Nick glanced quickly at Jessica, who was turning a deep shade of red. She sent Celine a murderous glance, which warmed Celine's heart. *It's your turn, Princess Jessica, to get a taste of unhappiness. You don't know what suffering is. Life has never mistreated you like it has me.*

Nick lightly held her wrist and inspected it. "It doesn't look broken, but I don't know if it's sprained or not. Maybe you should get it checked out by a doctor." Celine was standing so close that she got a whiff of his cologne. It was cool, spicy, and subtle. Some men didn't know how to wear scent; they went overboard or used the cheap stuff. But Nick obviously knew what he was doing. *He's a little hard edged, but with just enough class that I wouldn't be ashamed to be seen with him,* Celine thought with pleasure.

"Would you believe it's already starting to feel better? You must have the magic touch," she purred.

Jessica made a loud choking noise.

"Are you OK?" Nick asked politely, an amused gleam in his eye. He reached over to gently pat her on the back.

Jessica straightened and tossed back her mop of golden hair, her face tomato red. "I'm fine. Something just went down the wrong way."

Celine tittered behind her hand. "Oh, Jessica. You are just the funniest girl. I'm sooo glad you're going to be at Alison's party."

Jessica narrowed her eyes but smiled. "Why, thank you, Celine. I'm thrilled that you're thrilled, but I'm still not sure I'm free to attend."

"Speaking of the party," Alison broke in with an arch smile. "Celine and I would love to have you come, Nick. It's going to be at seven o'clock, very formal, very fun." She turned to Celine. "You can call Celine for the details. She's helping me set things up."

Celine whipped out a pen and ripped a sheet of paper from her notebook. "Here's my phone number. I can give you directions and anything else you need." She ignored the daggers Jessica was shooting at her as she fluttered her lashes at Nick. "I'll be moving soon, but you'll be able to reach me here for now."

Nick took the paper and folded it into his jeans pocket. "Great. Sounds like a good time. Doesn't it, Jessica?" He nudged her lightly in the ribs.

"Oh yeah, a really great time," Jessica said tightly. "But if you want to see the television set, Nick, I'll have to show it to you now. I have a class to go to."

Sure you do, Celine crowed to herself. *You just want to drag your prize away from us, or should I say away from me.*

"We really should be going too," Alison said.

As they exchanged good-byes Celine followed Alison away from Dickenson Hall, her mind a busy whirl. Things were going according to plan. Celine wouldn't have to be in exile from society much longer. Poor dead William White would no longer be ruining her life. It wasn't fair anyway. Just because William went a little crazy and tried to kill Princess Pill and her pathetic friends didn't mean Celine should have to suffer. After all, she was a victim too, and she was William's closest friend. Just because she helped him a little bit didn't mean she tried to kill anyone. Everyone seemed to have forgotten that William had tried to kill her.

William White would not be soon forgotten on the campus of SVU. Very rich, very handsome, and very crazy, William had ruled and terrorized for a long time. Even his incarceration in a mental institution hadn't kept the population safe. William had gone on a spree, first murdering an orderly, then trying to off Celine, and finally almost succeeding in murdering Elizabeth and all her closest friends.

The terror was over now. William White was dead, as dead as Celine's social life.

But Celine would soon be right back in the middle of things. In with the *crème de la crème* of SVU society, right where she belonged. And she'd be taking Nick Fox along with her. Stealing him away from Miss Jessica Wakefield would just be the cherry on the sundae.

Elizabeth crashed head-on with a tall body. The collision victim staggered from under his heavy backpack and gave her a dazed look.

"Sorry," Elizabeth murmured.

He just nodded and hurried away.

Elizabeth scolded herself for rushing absentmind-edly across campus. Especially during lunchtime, when she knew the walkways were brimming with students.

Immediately she was lost in thought again. Mr. Conroy was in a difficult predicament—it would be tragic if he didn't find his son. There had to be other records they could search, other resources they could tap into, Elizabeth mused to herself. If Mr. Conroy's son was here at Sweet Valley University, there had to be a means to find him.

She was so caught up in Mr. Conroy's problems, she was barely aware of making her way toward the cafeteria. *I'm an investigative reporter—I just have to put my mind to it. I have to think like a private investigator would.*

"Elizabeth. Hey, Liz, over here," a familiar male voice called from behind her as she approached the cafeteria doors.

Elizabeth turned, surprised. "Todd Wilkins. I can't believe it. I thought you had dropped off the face of the earth." A warm smile lit up her face.

Todd was a good friend now, but it hadn't always been that way. He and Elizabeth had been high-school sweethearts, and both had assumed they would remain a couple forever. But the strains of col-lege life had torn them apart, and Todd had hurt her terribly. That was all behind them now, and they each had a new, steady love in their lives.

45

"Where've you been these days? Busy with Gin-Yung?"

Todd shifted the huge load of books in his arms and opened the door. They walked into the lobby. "No. Actually Gin-Yung and I are taking a break from each other." At Elizabeth's concerned expression he shook his head. "It's not what you think. Gin-Yung's been offered a great opportunity. She's abroad this semester, in London. She received a paid internship with a big newspaper in the city. She's going to report on major soccer tournaments. You know, soccer's the hot sport in Europe." Todd smiled, genuine pride shining in his eyes.

Elizabeth was momentarily taken aback. Gin-Yung Suh was a wonderful girl, bright, feisty, and totally in love with Todd. As a matter of fact, the two of them seemed to be the perfect couple. As she and Todd settled into chairs, Elizabeth gave herself a mental shake. If the two of them were happy with the situation, that was all that mattered.

"I'm glad for Gin-Yung. That sounds like a great opportunity. How does she feel about taking a break from you?" Elizabeth knew only too well how much it hurt to be dumped by someone you loved and trusted.

Todd was quick to respond. "Gin-Yung is absolutely fine with it. Surprisingly, we both decided separately before we even discussed it that this would be for the best. We're young, and we don't want to mess things up by getting tied down too fast and getting distracted from our career plans."

"Well, if you two are content, then who am I to say anything?" Elizabeth smiled and shrugged, flicking her blond ponytail back over her shoulder.

Todd nodded as he stacked his books beside him. "It's not only that long-distance relationships don't work, Liz. I think we both needed the break. Plus I have some incredible news myself." He looked up, his eyes glowing with excitement. "I'm back on the basketball team!"

"Todd! That's excellent. You deserve it after all you went through," Elizabeth shouted. She high-fived him and grinned broadly. "With the athletics department cleaned up, the team should really go to the top this season." She and Todd exchanged satisfied looks. They shared a personal history of taking on the previously corrupt athletics department and exposing its involvement with mobster alumnus T. Clay Santos and his gambling scheme. Players had been paid to lose, and money for the department had been siphoned into the point-shaving scam.

Todd had been a star basketball player but had been kicked off the team when his acceptance of certain gifts and favors was revealed in an exposé by Elizabeth and Tom. Neither Tom nor Elizabeth had known then that Todd would be a victim of the fall-out. Todd had been overwhelmed as a new freshman, excited by all the attention and superstar treatment he received.

The adulation had gone to his head, making his

comedown all the more painful. Since then he had taken his licks and had grown up considerably. He'd also had an extremely long run of bad breaks, everything from being the athletics department's scapegoat to being framed for various crimes by the late William White. His struggle to reclaim his self-esteem had been a hard one.

"I know, I can't believe it. But that's why I'm kind of glad that Gin-Yung and I can have this separation. Now I can totally concentrate on my game and my studies. I need to make up for lost time. I want to raise my GPA and keep my game at its best." His expression grew serious. "I've been down and out for a while now, Liz. I've felt like a real loser. This is my chance to better my life, to show everyone and myself that I can be a success again."

Elizabeth looked disturbed. "You've never been a loser, Todd. I admit you've had a rough time lately, but you can't blame yourself for everything." She leaned forward, her voice earnest. "You've been responsible for many positive things too. You saved us all from William White. You helped expose the problems in the athletics department. Gin-Yung saw what a great guy you are and fell in love with you. You have to give yourself some credit."

"I hear what you're saying, but I still haven't felt right about myself in a long time. I feel like I finally have a chance to make something of myself, and I want to take it. Eliminating romance and relationship stuff from my life will make it easier to accomplish my goals," he continued intently.

His handsome face was deadly serious, and Elizabeth felt a pang of sympathy. She herself had had a rough beginning as a freshman at SVU. Of course, Todd had been a major part of her troubles, but she couldn't blame it all on him. Her own insecurity and fears had led her to make unfortunate decisions, which she had dearly paid for. Overeating, dating William White, and mistrusting Tom Watts were just a few of her mistakes. Her stomach knotted momentarily before she reminded herself that the past was past.

It was time for Todd also to put it all behind him. Squaring her jaw, Elizabeth spoke forcefully. "Todd, I really believe you are going to reach your goals. I know you, and I know what you can do once you put your mind to something." She felt a warm surge of pride for him.

Todd stood. "Thanks for the vote of confidence, Liz, but I better get going. Anyway, I'm glad I ran into you." He gathered up his books. "I have to go to bio lab. I take it you're meeting Tom for lunch?"

She nodded and watched as he threw a half wave and walked out the door. She and Todd had finally done it. They'd grown up. It seemed as if they'd left the major heartaches and miseries behind them. Now they could concentrate on just being happy. Life would be tranquil; the traumas of the past were behind them.

* * *

Nick Fox was in trouble. One hour with a blond dynamo named Jessica and he was almost forgetting his mission. It wasn't his fault. Even the hard-core guys he knew would have melted in the presence of Jessica Wakefield.

Jessica couldn't walk two feet without being stopped by someone calling out hello or asking her what her plans were for the weekend. Yet she was perfectly nonchalant about the attention.

Nick, meanwhile, had to stay alert. There was too much going on. People were flowing in and out of Jessica's dorm. All kinds of people. For instance, Nick thought that big, husky guy standing by the exit was acting a little strangely until he realized that the guy was just delivering a pizza.

Looking up at him with her wicked blue-green eyes, Jessica couldn't stop teasing him about his success with Celine and Alison. "Alison Quinn only invites the few select people she deems worthy of her company. She hardly *ever* warms up to strangers and *never* invites them to her parties, not unless she has a personal dossier on them." Her eyes twinkled as she glided gracefully beside him. "You're either a magician or . . ." She narrowed her eyes at him appraisingly.

"Or I just happened to be in the right place at the right time," Nick cut in with a skeptical smile. He really had to watch himself around this young woman. Not only was she beautiful, but outrageously charming. And Nick knew that kind of charm was dangerous. He was already distracted.

"Hi, Jessica!" a small brunette sang out ahead of them.

Jessica waved. "Hi, Ashley." The brunette waved and smiled before disappearing into her dorm room.

"My room is 28—it's just down the hallway," Jessica said, pointing.

"If your fans will ever let us get there, that is," Nick teased. He enjoyed watching Jessica's expressive face.

"Fans—right!" Jessica said, wrinkling her nose. "Most of them are mere acquaintances. It's easy to find people to be friendly with—what's hard is to find someone you really click with." She sent him a glance from under her long lashes.

Nick felt his blood rush through his veins in response. *Cool it, Fox,* he warned himself. *Remember why you're here.*

"Here we are." Jessica opened the door and motioned him inside. "Let me tell you something about Celine. She only likes the handsomest and richest men at SVU," Jessica informed him.

Nick followed her in. "Hmmm, seems like she blew it on both counts with me."

Jessica tossed back her hair. "If you're fishing for compliments, you'll have to go back to Celine or Alison," she retorted.

"Your two favorite people," Nick said wryly. It was obvious as the butter yellow paint on the wall that those two girls were deathly jealous of Jessica, and with good cause.

"Let's just say they like me about as much as I like them," Jessica answered neatly.

Nick stopped in his tracks in wide-eyed amazement. Slowly he surveyed Jessica's room, which was a portrait of contradictions. One side was immaculate, flawlessly neat. The other side looked like a volcano had erupted beneath a mountain of clothes, books, and papers.

Jessica caught his expression. "This half of the room is my sister, Elizabeth's. She's the serious, studious type," she explained, pointing to the tidy half. "And this side"—she pointed dramatically—"is mine. I'm more the creative type. And you know what they say, 'Talent and messiness go hand in hand.'"

Nick chuckled. Jessica was gorgeous *and* funny, a unique combination. "Well, if that's what *they* say, then it must be true."

"Besides, my sister is older and more concerned about appearances," Jessica added.

"How much older is she?" Nick picked up a stuffed rabbit inches from his feet and handed it to Jessica.

"OK—I confess. She's not that much older. We're identical twins, but she *was* born four minutes ahead of me." Jessica threw him a naughty smile and tossed the rabbit onto her bed.

"Twins!" Nick shook his head. There couldn't be two Jessicas, of that he was sure. "That's amazing. Let me guess—you two are total opposites." He nodded at the room, with its immaculate and messy halves.

"You guessed right. My sister is completely different from me. All she does is study and worry about fixing the world's problems. She hardly ever does anything just for fun." Jessica shook her head and bent down to scoop up a robe crumpled on the floor. "Can you imagine how dull her life is?"

"You and she really don't sound like you have much in common," was Nick's diplomatic comment.

Jessica jutted out her chin. "We are close, though, and always will be. Twins have a special relationship. Here," she said, motioning toward the perfectly made bed. "You can sit on Liz's bed. She won't mind. I'll get the TV."

Golden hair swinging, Jessica strode toward the closet and flung it open.

This girl was quite a find. While she wasn't exactly the type he was looking for—and Nick had radarlike instincts when it came to reading people— she would be perfect as a connection. Business, he reminded himself. He was here for business. She would be able to introduce him to the kind of people he was seeking. Jessica was obviously a popular girl, a member of the hottest sorority, and she was liked by nearly everyone.

"Ta-da!" Jessica emerged from the closet and thrust the TV set before him with a flourish. "Here it is, the bargain of a lifetime." She threw him a guilty smile. "I'm only joking, of course."

Nick looked at the set and gulped. It looked old and pretty battered. "Well," he said with what he hoped was optimism. "Let's plug it in." *Maybe it's not as bad as it appears,* he told himself. Maybe Jessica had exaggerated.

They watched as the eye-cramping screen filled with a fuzzy picture. Jessica jiggled the knobs and fiddled with the antenna, but the few horizontal lines still bounced up and down.

Jessica pounded on top of the television, but the fuzziness and lines remained.

She looked downcast. "I guess you don't want it. I told you it wasn't that great, but I shouldn't have even put up the ad," she added sorrowfully, courageously looking him in the eye. "Elizabeth told me I should be more honest. Actually I stretched the truth when I said I was selling the TV because Elizabeth needs the money. She thought we should give it to a junkyard."

Elizabeth, you were right on the money. I don't know anything else about you, but you do know TV sets, Nick mused to himself. Aloud he said, "Don't look so glum. People do what they have to when making a sale. Besides, I just want the set for listening to the news and for background noise. I hardly ever look at the screen, so your TV is just fine." He carried the set to the door and turned toward Jessica, who was staring at him openmouthed. "One hundred dollars seems like a fair price to me." He pulled out his wallet and peeled out five twenties. "You're in luck. I just went to the ATM machine. Normally this bill-fold's pretty flat." He grinned at her and handed her the money.

A small price to pay in the long run, he reassured himself. *Especially if I get what I want. And I have to admit, Jessica is a hard woman to say no to.*

Jessica fumbled with the bills for a second, her eyes huge with disbelief, before scurrying to her desk drawer.

Nick hid a grin at her expression.

Thrusting the money inside and slamming the drawer shut, Jessica spun around. "I don't know what to say except thanks. You're a very sweet guy, Nick Fox." Her cheeks were pink as she boldly met his eyes.

"Sweet? I wouldn't go that far," he joked, ignoring the twinge of discomfort he was suddenly feeling. "But if you really want to thank me, why don't you go out with me tonight?"

"I would love to. Now that you're the new owner of our old TV, we're practically related," Jessica suggested saucily.

She was standing so near, he could smell the delicious scent of her hair. Her lips were invitingly close. All he had to do was take one step closer. . . .

Nick gave himself a mental kick. *Don't forget, Fox, you've got business to attend to. Get your hormones under control.*

Nick laughed and slung the TV set under his arm. "Buying this old TV may pay off after all—but I better leave before you decide to sell me your old toaster or your broken hot plate." *She could probably sell me anything,* he thought ruefully.

Jessica giggled and reached to open the door for him. "Elizabeth always says I can talk anybody into anything."

"I believe it. I'll see you tonight, then, Miss Wakefield," Nick said. He turned halfway out the door. "By the way, dress casual."

With one last look at her lovely face, he clicked the door behind him. Nick sighed and walked down the hall to the exit. He had to remind himself that Jessica Wakefield was not his main objective; she was just a means to an end. He shouldn't have been so excited that she'd agreed to go out with him. She was merely a connection and nothing more.

Now he just needed to convince his racing heart and rattled nerves of that fact.

Chapter Three

"He's such a nice man, Tom. He cares so deeply about finding his son. I know there's an incredible story behind Mr. Conroy's search. I can just feel it," Elizabeth enthused. She paused to sip her glass of skim milk and then scooped up a forkful of salad. Ignoring the limp lettuce drooping over her fork, she bubbled on. "When I first met Mr. Conroy, I was really upset that they wouldn't give me credit for my Outreach internship. But getting involved with his cause has put it all in perspective. Battling for credits seems so trivial compared to Mr. Conroy finding the son he's never met."

Tom was staring dull eyed and using his fork to poke at the burrito on his plate. All around them the cafeteria buzzed and hummed. The air was thick with smells of onions and burnt hot dogs.

Elizabeth gently touched his arm. "Is something wrong?"

"Huh?" Tom looked up, startled. "Did you say something, Elizabeth?"

Elizabeth bit back an irritated retort. Obviously something was bothering Tom. He was normally sensitive and attentive. She shrugged. "I was just rambling. I'm more concerned about what's going on with you."

Tom sighed heavily and rolled the Tabasco bottle between his fingers. "I don't know. I don't want to dump my bad mood on you." His thick lashes hid his eyes from her.

"What are girlfriends for but to dump your moods on?" Elizabeth smiled at him.

Tom was a naturally reserved person, but he wasn't usually prone to mood swings. She'd never seen him so down. His handsome face was drawn, and she felt a real surge of worry. Elizabeth always considered Tom to be one of the steadiest people she knew. She found it hard to believe that briefly in his past he was "Wildman Watts," the guy who'd partied and strutted his stuff with the other jocks. He was typically so strong and confident. It was painful to see him so shaken and unhappy.

Tom rubbed his forehead wearily. "My birthday's this Saturday, as you know, and I can't bear the thought of it. Lately I've been thinking about my family—how they died—and how much I miss them. It seems unfair that they won't be around for my twenty-first birthday. They would have loved sharing it with me, Liz. How can I celebrate without them?"

Elizabeth felt an ache deep in her heart. She knew the loss of Tom's family had left deep scars and that he missed them very much. But she hadn't ever seen him this disturbed. Tom looked so sad and tired. She wished she could lighten his mood by telling him about the surprise party she was planning for him on Saturday night. All their friends would be there.

Elizabeth was putting together a tremendous celebration, the kind people would talk about for years after. It would be a night that would stick in Tom's mind forever. Elizabeth was convinced that the festivities and the warmth and affection from all their friends would boost his spirits. She sighed to herself. Of course, she couldn't tell him now and spoil the surprise.

"I'm sorry, Tom. All I can say is that lots of people care about you—especially me. I only wish—"

Tom interrupted her, changing the subject swiftly. "Thanks, I appreciate that. So what was that exciting new story you were telling me about?" He snapped his fingers. "Oh yeah, some guy you met in the bursar's office had lost his kid's grades or something. . . ."

Elizabeth tried not to wince. Mr. Conroy was the last topic Tom needed to hear about. The way Tom was feeling about his own family, Mr. Conroy's situation would only depress him more. Elizabeth took a teasing approach. "Hey, I thought you weren't even listening. Do you have another set of ears that I don't know about?" She reached across to ruffle his hair. "I always knew you had extra-thick hair—maybe it's so you can hide that second pair of ears."

Tom gave a faint smile. "No, I've just learned to listen while my mind's on other things, a great skill for the classroom. But seriously, you know I'm always interested in what you have to say. I'm sorry I'm so out of it." His dark eyes searched hers with the tenderness she loved. "Am I forgiven?"

Elizabeth grinned and reached across to tap his plate. "Yup, but only if you'll share some of that *mucho* delicious-looking burrito."

Tom pushed the plate with its white leaden-looking burrito toward her. "Gladly," he said with a small smile. "It's all yours, with my condolences."

Elizabeth chuckled and moved the plate away. "That bad, huh? Why don't you go get a sandwich or a slice of pizza?"

"I'm not hungry. I'll grab something later," he said, running his hands through his hair. "So you were telling me about this story. . . ."

Boy, Tom is like a pit bull when he scents something important. He just doesn't give up. Elizabeth stifled a groan, wishing for a distraction. Since fate wasn't on her side, she struggled to come up with a believable excuse.

"Actually, Tom, there really isn't a story yet. Just the seed of one. When I . . . uh, find out more details, I'll know if there's anything to tell. But for now . . ." Elizabeth stammered, nervously licking her lips. When Tom stared at her like that, she felt as if she were going to be frisked any minute. She took a long gulp of milk, which was warm by now. Making a face, she pushed it back.

"OK, I understand," he said, his eyes scanning her face intently. "I have an idea. Why don't we have dinner tonight and make up for this pathetic lunch? How about Pizza Paradiso?"

"Yum—I deserve some decent pizza after suffering through this salad. Sometimes I think they should condemn this cafeteria or charge the cooks with cruel and unusual punishment." She stared down at her half-empty bowl of soggy greens. "I love Pizza Paradiso, as long as we don't have to try Danny's favorite, pineapple pizza. I'll stick with pepperoni." Elizabeth patted her growling stomach. "I can hardly wait."

Tom rose and reached across to give her a quick kiss. "Well, I have to go, Liz. Are you going to stick around here?"

She nodded and gave him a quick peck good-bye. "I have to look over some notes before my next class. I thought I'd get a diet soda too." Elizabeth watched Tom trudge past the tables of chattering diners and out through the doors. Someone called out to him, but he didn't seem to hear and moved on as if in a trance. Apparently she hadn't bolstered him up one bit.

Elizabeth swept up their dishes and trash and deposited them quickly. Tom usually cleaned up after

61

himself; this was just another hint of how down he was. Hurrying through the food line, Elizabeth filled her glass with a diet soft drink and paused. She frowned.

She had to keep Tom away from the sensitive George Conroy story and she had to keep the surprise party a surprise. Keeping one secret was bad enough, but two would be impossible. Tom Watts was just too good at digging out the truth.

"You guys will never believe it!" Jessica Wakefield shouted, flinging open the doors to the Theta house parlor room. "Never in a million years."

Two pairs of eyes, one gray and one blue, studied her with mock confusion.

Isabella Ricci leaned her chin on her palm and looked thoughtful. "Let me guess—you've been chosen to study under the chess maestro of SVU, the brilliant Albert Ludvig."

"No, that's not it, Iz," Lila Fowler interjected smoothly. "Jessica has chosen to take a vow of silence and is joining the Sweet Valley monastery." Lila ran her fingers idly through her long brown hair, a thoughtful expression on her face. "We all know how Jessica has grown so introspective these days and how she absolutely disdains fashion. I can see our Jess now in a plain brown robe—"

"Very funny, you guys," Jessica said, tapping her foot impatiently and rolling her eyes.

"Lila, we've got it all wrong. Jessica is signing up

to live in the Emerson Scholastic House—you know, the one for honor students only," Isabella gasped, her gray eyes wide.

"Or could it be," Lila suggested, turning a serious expression toward Isabella, "that this announcement involves a *man?*"

Isabella shook her head in exaggerated amazement. "Our Jessica interested in a man—never!"

Isabella and Lila finally lost control and burst into gales of laughter at Jessica's outraged expression. They rolled around on the couch they were lounging on and stopped only to wipe away the tears running down their cheeks. They choked and sputtered but still fought back more blasts of giggles. Finally they calmed down, coughing and smoothing their hair.

Jessica plopped down on the nearest chair and reached for the plate of scones and brioches resting on top of the gleaming coffee table. "You two are so hilarious," she said dryly. "Why don't I call you Groucho and Harpo? Or better yet, Heckle and Jeckle?" She sank her teeth into a cinnamon-raisin scone and caught the crumbs in a neatly pressed linen napkin. Theta house offered so many pleasant perks, like linen napkins and a real tea service. Theta house had style and class, more so than any other sorority house. Just sitting there, surrounded by all its stately charm, was enough to soothe Jessica.

"I'm sorry, Jess." Isabella smoothed down her already perfect dark hair. "You're so easy to tease. But honestly, I want to hear your news." She was, as usual, attired in the most elegant of fashions, a sleek shell set in cranberry silk twill, which highlighted her creamy complexion.

Lila looked up from the hand mirror she was holding. "Me too." She frowned as she switched from pearl teardrop earrings to tiny diamond-studded gold hoops.

"I met the most gorgeous, fascinating man today," Jessica began eagerly. Pouring herself a cup of tea from the silver teapot, she told them the entire saga of how she had met Nick at the student center and how he'd bought her and Elizabeth's cruddy old TV set. She also told them about the way he avoided telling her anything about himself. She just loved a mystery man.

"If he bought that old set, he's probably not financially secure. He might even be in desperate straits," Lila warned. She carefully set the pearl earrings down on the table. Lila had been born to money and rarely thought about the cost of things. She was used to the best, and her jewelry was never costume but always the genuine article.

"Lots of students are poor," Isabella commented, ever practical. "What's strange is how he didn't want to tell you anything personal about himself."

"First of all, he spent a hundred dollars in cash, so he can't be exactly poor," Jessica argued heatedly. "Second of all, I wouldn't care if he was. Third of all, he told me plenty about himself."

"Never trust a man who carries that much cash around," intoned Lila.

"Name one single fact that you know about this guy," Isabella demanded.

"His name," Jessica cried triumphantly. "Nick Fox." She smiled at her two friends smugly. She was not going to let them spoil her pleasure with their dreary, old-lady fussiness. Just because in the past she'd made several mistakes in the romance department, everyone assumed she had no judgment.

Isabella shook her head. "That's pretty lame, Jess."

Lila was tugging off the diamond hoops. "I have to agree. A name doesn't tell you much."

"Well, I'll find out all I need to know tonight." Jessica preened. "We're going out on a date. Then I can report back to you two nervous Nellies." Jessica hugged herself with glee. Not that she'd report everything. The juicy stuff would remain private. *I'll tell them the basic stats only. Just the facts, ma'am.* She giggled out loud.

"I hope it works out," Isabella said generously. "And that he turns out to be everything you want him to be."

"Enough about Jessica and her mystery man. What I want to know is which earrings look best with this outfit?" Lila began, holding out both pairs.

Isabella leaned forward with appraising eyes. She touched the pearl earrings with one flawlessly manicured fingernail. "The pearls. Definitely the pearls."

Jessica nodded in absent agreement.

"That's what I thought," Lila said, putting on the earrings. She poured more tea into each of their cups.

Jessica lowered her voice significantly and looked from Isabella to Lila. "Listen, there's more news. You won't believe who I ran into. . . ." She set down her teacup and proceeded to tell them about her encounter with Alison and Celine. "Isn't that bizarre and creepy?" Jessica raised her brows expressively. "Those two together—it gives me the shivers. Besides, what kind of surprise could Alison be planning?"

"All I know is that she invited me," Isabella said. "Beyond that, I'm as much in the dark as you. What about you, Lila?"

Lila shrugged. "She invited me too, but I don't know anything about Alison's surprise either."

"Why don't you ask Alison herself?" came a fourth voice, startling the three of them.

Alison Quinn, vice president of the Thetas, paraded through the parlor with a prissy little smile on her face.

Jessica covered a grimace. It was just like Alison to be lurking behind closed doors. Jessica wondered how much Alison had overheard. She couldn't have heard everything, Jessica decided, or she would be seething with outrage.

Alison seated herself like royalty and reached for a brioche. She bared her teeth in a wide smile at the three girls. "I promise that you won't be disappointed with my surprise. Even you, Jessica, shouldn't have any complaints."

Isabella spoke quickly. "Why don't you clue us in, Alison? After all, we are sisters."

Lila nodded. "Maybe we can help you with your surprise. If it's that big, Alison, you don't want to handle it on your own."

"I'm not," Alison said with delight. She tossed back her straight brown hair. "Celine and I are working on this together."

"Celine!" they all cried at once. The three of them exchanged pointed looks.

Celine again, thought Jessica in disgust. That girl kept turning up like a bad virus. Alison had acted earlier as if Celine were only helping her set up the party; now she was hinting that Celine was in on the surprise. The two were tighter than Jessica had realized.

Alison smirked and shook her head. "I can't divulge anything, or it would ruin the surprise for everyone."

"Alison, really. Why all the suspense?" Lila asked coolly.

Alison took a long sip of tea before answering. *She's just playing with us,* Jessica seethed to herself. Queen Bee enjoying all the attention.

"Celine and I will make it worth the wait. You'll see," Alison said complacently.

"Celine?" Isabella repeated with a raised eyebrow.

"You will all be surprised at how generous Celine is. The girl has turned over a new leaf." Alison turned to look meaningfully at Lila and Isabella. Jessica, she ignored. "You'll understand everything at my dinner tomorrow. Don't miss it, or you'll really be sorry," she added archly. "I won't say another word. My lips are sealed."

Don't we all wish they really were, Jessica thought in disgust. The conversation soon changed to other topics. Jessica wished that Alison would leave, but as luck would have it, she was planted in her chair as if she'd taken root. Jessica broke another scone in two, wishing she could toss a piece at Alison's mouth, which was moving incessantly again.

"Don't you think this old parlor could use a face-lift—a more modern look?" Alison said lazily. She waved her hand around the room. "The furnishings in here are really getting shabby and worn."

Isabella and Lila nodded simultaneously and eagerly began to throw decorating ideas back and forth. They were so excited that Jessica thought the two of them were going to bounce right off the sofa and onto the floor.

"I see something in a desert motif." Isabella narrowed her eyes. "Southwestern but not too kitschy—no hokey fake skulls or imitation Georgia O'Keefes. The colors should be warm, lots of sand and rose."

"Hmmm," Lila interjected. "I was seeing something Edwardian, with lots of cool colors, blues, lavenders. Furniture—plush but not overdone . . ."

Jessica began tuning them out. The two of them could go on and on forever about fabrics. Besides, Lila—who was used to the finest—and Isabella—who breathed fashion—were creating a *House Beautiful* parlor, which would probably cost in the tens of thousands.

Jessica herself had been about to object to Alison's suggestion almost as a reflex. But after studying the elegant old room, she got excited about the idea of beautifying it. Her ideas were more realistic than Lila's and Isabella's. She envisioned modern decor, something stark but dramatic. Jessica smiled, thinking about it.

Proposals for the renovations grew more fantastic and more expensive, and the girls grew more animated. *What's the harm in fantasizing?* Jessica thought. They could never afford to make all those changes, but it was fun to pretend.

Alex scowled down at her plate of french fries. The ketchup-covered potato sticks seemed to be smirking at her, as if to say, "Nah, nah, even we could have aced that Western philosophy exam."

At least her professor hadn't accused her of cheating. He had provided her with an extra pen, even though his expression had been as sour as month-old milk.

Unfortunately the pen wasn't magic and it didn't help Alex remember any of the answers.

She leaned her chin in her hands and closed her

eyes. Why was it now that she remembered "Occam's razor"? Now, when it was too late. "Occam's razor" was easy: "Do not multiply entities beyond necessity." Or in layman's terms—when you have two hypotheses to choose from, pick the simpler one. Alex had written down that "Occam's razor" had something to do with math, which was not only totally wrong but completely pathetic.

Face it, Alexandra Rollins, you failed the exam, she chastised herself cruelly. Images of the test, with all her wrong answers written on it, floated through her brain. She had studied so hard and long, but she knew a big, fat F was waiting for her. The word *loser* flashed like neon in her mind. Alex's stomach bolted and rebelled. The lights above were suddenly harsh and garish, and Alex could imagine how pale and washed out she must look under them.

Noah reached across the table and tapped her arm. "Hey, earth to Alex. Come in, do you read me?" he teased.

"I read you, loud and clear," Alex grumbled, thrusting her turkey club sandwich away from her. With another sweep of her hand, the plate of fries followed.

"Aren't you hungry? That club looks pretty good. Can I have a bite?" Noah was lanky but had an enormous appetite. His plate of nachos was already demolished.

Alex nodded. "Go ahead—my stomach feels like a lead balloon." She wadded her napkin with more force than necessary.

Noah bit into the sandwich and gazed across the table at her, his eyes behind his glasses bright and sharp. The snack bar was almost empty now. Alex and Noah were dining late, and only a few stragglers filled the surrounding tables. Eating was the last thing Alex wanted to do, but Noah had been persistent. She and Noah Pearson were a couple and usually did things together, but tonight Alex wished she could be alone. She didn't know if she could stand telling Noah that she failed her exam. He would give her a pep talk, which in her present mood would only make her scream.

"Maybe you should eat something. You might be having a drop in your blood sugar. That can make you tired and irritable, you know."

"I'm fine," Alex said, brushing her auburn hair from her face. "Don't worry, Noah, I won't starve. And I'm not irritable!"

"Hey, speaking of worrying—did I tell you the good news?" He was beaming so broadly, Alex thought his cheeks might crack. "You know how I was really concerned about getting into that advanced clinical psychology class—the one for upperclassmen. Well, I got the word today from Professor Majoris that I've been accepted." Noah paused to take a drink of cola. "Anyway, he said that my grades and intern experience qualified me as a special case. So I'm in." He looked expectantly across the table at Alex.

She worked up a feeble smile. "Great, Noah."

71

He's in and I might be out—out of college completely if I keep failing exams.

"Actually today was a pretty busy day. Professor Wolfe asked me to be his teaching assistant next semester, which would include payment and credits," Noah added casually. "I told him I'd have to think about it. I need to make sure my schedule isn't too tight."

Alex bobbed her head and smiled, feeling like a marionette. "That's really great," she repeated. *You sound like a stupid echo,* she told herself. She barely listened as Noah went on to tell her how great his day had been and fought back a wave of resentment. Gazing from under her lashes at his handsome, absorbed face, she felt a stab of sharp annoyance. *Everything comes so easily for Noah. He just takes it as his due. I wonder how calm and cheerful he'd be if he ever failed at anything.*

He was smiling steadily at her, and Alex squirmed in discomfort. "What is it? Why are you looking at me like that?"

"I was just thinking how proud I am of you, Alex. You've come such a long way from when we first talked on the campus hot line." Alex had initially met Noah over the telephone. He had used the pseudonym T-Squared and had counseled her anonymously through a rocky time in her life. Neither of them had realized that they shared a class together and that the two people who were attracted to each other in class were the same two people who liked each other over the phone. It had taken them both a while to figure it all out.

Sometimes Alex was nostalgic when she thought of those old days with T-Squared, the kind but mysterious stranger. At least T-Squared had been passionately responsive to Alex's every mood and emotion. Their involvement had been a real roller-coaster ride for them both. In the beginning everything between Noah and Alex had been so intense and dramatic.

"It's no easy thing to get sober," Noah continued seriously. "But you did it, and you really turned your life around. You're making remarkable progress, Alex. You should be as proud as I am."

Noah's words scraped at her nerves and electrified within her a sudden bolt of anger. T-Squared would have never sounded so pompous. *Making remarkable progress*—what right did he have to judge her? Sure, she felt like a loser, but he didn't have to rub it in. Noah was only studying psychology. He wasn't a real psychologist, after all. Why didn't he just pat her on the head and be done with it? Another patronizing comment from him and she would explode.

Alex leapt to her feet and grabbed her purse.

Noah just stared at her. Naturally he didn't seem to have a clue. He would keep on babbling, and they'd end up in a fight. Despite everything, Alex didn't want that.

"I'm feeling kind of sick," she interrupted. "I feel

a headache starting. I need to go home and rest, Noah."

He started to get up, but she waved him down. "You stay and finish eating, really. I'm not good company now."

"What about Alison's dinner tomorrow night? Will you be up to it?" Noah gave her a concerned look.

He acts like I'm some kind of invalid, she thought, gritting her teeth. "I'll be fine by tomorrow. Call me later, OK?" She forced a tiny smile and rushed off before she started yelling or crying.

Alex walked slowly back to her room. The night air was cool, stirred by a gentle breeze. Couples who seemed obscenely happy and carefree passed her, depressing her further.

She had a sickening feeling that her old precollege self was taking over, that she was turning back into high-school Enid—the Enid who'd been a boring, invisible nobody.

When she had first changed her name to Alexandra, she had changed her image too. Alex initially had been very happy at SVU, thrilled with her new, glamorous, exciting life. Then everything had crashed down around her. It had taken gut-wrenching work to turn her life around and still hang on to those Alex qualities that she liked, such as being more outgoing and fashion conscious. Alex, at least, was her own person, not some pathetic little mouse like Enid had been.

74

Now it was all slipping away, and the old Enid self seemed to be taking over, like some creepy alien from *Invasion of the Body Snatchers*.

Alex's head really had begun to pound; actually, her whole body had. The world demanded too much from Alexandra Rollins. She knew of only one thing that could make the stress and misery go away. The one thing she absolutely could not have was the one thing she craved. A cold, soothing shot of alcohol.

Chapter Four

"I'll just die if Tom finds out." Elizabeth tightened her jaw with determination as she reached back to undo her ponytail. "I won't let Tom spoil his own surprise party." She shook out her hair and wearily massaged her temples. Planning a party was hard work.

Curled up on her bed, Elizabeth reread her list. It was getting late, and her stomach was growling for pizza. Flipping through the pages of her legal pad, she was positive that she hadn't forgotten anything. Tom's surprise party was going to go off without a hitch.

Let's see, I've taken care of the food, drinks, and the room to hold the party in. I have Tom's gift. The guest list is complete. Danny, Nina, Bryan, and Winston have all agreed to help me set this up, and they're totally psyched for it. All I have to do is keep Tom from finding out. Elizabeth looked up and nibbled on her pen with a faint frown. She could keep the party a secret. It should be as easy as a piece of frosted birthday cake.

She blew the blond bangs out of her eyes and leaned back against the pillows. *Whew, time for a break*. Elizabeth reached for her can of diet cola and took a long drink.

Tom's party was going to be well worth all the effort. If his surprise party didn't cheer him up, nothing would. Elizabeth smiled to herself, picturing all their friends filling the room and shouting, "Surprise!" and Tom, amazed but happy that so many people cared about him.

Tom had a bad case of the blues, but she had the cure. Elizabeth set her soda can down and returned to her pad. She was determined to make this party a blast. Carefully she read down the page again.

Suddenly the door flew open. Elizabeth jumped and gasped, knocking her pen to the floor. "Tom! What are you doing here? You're early!" Frantically she stuffed the notepad under her pillow.

"I didn't mean to startle you. I guess I was in a hurry and forgot to knock," he said as he shut the door behind him. Tom strode across the room and scooped up the pen. "Here, you dropped this." He was towering over her.

Elizabeth grabbed it and peered up at him uneasily.

"You seem nervous, Liz. Is something going on?"

Just then Elizabeth noticed that the edge of the notepad was peeking out from under the pillow. She forced her eyes away. "Of course <u>not</u>." She faked a laugh. "I'm just starving. I could eat a whole pizza myself."

"Hmmm." He crossed his arms in front of his chest. "I could have sworn I just saw you hide something under your pillow."

Elizabeth bit back a groan. Tom was impossible. He noticed absolutely everything. Elizabeth got up and slipped her arms around his waist. He was incredibly handsome and smelled delicious too. She brushed her lips softly against his. "I'm also hungry for your kisses," she whispered huskily. "If I go too long without them, I get a little lightheaded." She fluttered her lashes.

Tom responded warmly, and Elizabeth felt relief ooze through her veins. She was out of the woods. The kiss grew more passionate, and Elizabeth started to forget all about her subterfuge . . . and the party . . . and everything. . . .

Until Tom pulled back and scrutinized her face. "Wait a minute," he said, breathing a little fast. "That sounded more like something Jess would say. What gives, Liz?"

Elizabeth paused a moment to catch her breath. "I don't know what you're talking about." She widened her blue-green eyes at him. "I sounded like Jessica? I think I'm insulted." She dimpled up at him.

He frowned.

Elizabeth sighed. "Aren't you here to feed me, Tom? I don't think I can wait another minute." She silently pleaded with him to take the bait. Still standing only inches away from him, Elizabeth gazed up with a hungry expression.

Tom took a determined step back. "We'll go eat," he declared. "As soon as you tell me what's really going on here. . . ."

I'm cool. I'm in control. I'm focused, Nick Fox reassured himself. He stole a look at Jessica's perfect, lovely face and felt his insides quiver.

Nick pulled up into a huge gravel lot, spinning the wheels of his gleaming 1967 black Camaro. The sun was sinking with a fanfare of colors, turning the horizon a fiery orange. Several yards away lights flashed, people screamed, and horns blared. He smiled down at Jessica.

"I hope you like carnivals, Jessica. My intuition tells me that you and I are a lot alike—that you crave action and excitement, and that you're just a little kid at heart."

Jessica looked up at him with sparkling eyes. "You've got me pegged. I'm *always* ready for excitement. I can never get enough." She bounced in her seat, as if really happy about his choice of entertainment. Jessica Wakefield looked more delectable than he'd remembered, and Nick had thought he had every detail of her imprinted on his brain. In narrow black jeans and a white midriff halter, she looked stunning and sexy. Too sexy for his peace of mind. The wind blew through the rolled-down windows and stirred a strand of golden hair across her face. She was wearing her long hair clipped to one side. Nick fought the temptation to undo the barrette and release the silken mane. Instead he reached and gently moved the hair out of her eyes.

They smiled silently at each other and climbed out of the car. Nick made a mock bow. "Shall we, fellow thrill seeker?"

Jessica laughed in delight and waited while he secured the windows and locked the doors. Nick took her arm and led her across the rough, unpaved ground.

Sunshine Carnival was small, filled with traditional rides and exhibits. Families with little children, teenagers, and couples holding hands milled around, eating cotton candy, corn dogs, and ice cream. Mouthwatering scents of buttery popcorn and frying sausages drifted across the grounds. Loud shrieks and wild laughter filled the air as Jessica and Nick strolled past the rides.

"I don't know about you," Nick said, "but I could use some chow. You're not a health-food nut, are you?"

Jessica shook her head. "No way. Especially not when there's great junk food around."

The concession stands were clustered at one end of the fairgrounds. Jessica, Nick discovered, had a cast-iron stomach when it came to munching down hot dogs, snow cones, and cotton candy. He appreciated a hearty appetite in a woman.

With their hunger satisfied, Nick and Jessica drifted toward the rides. Nick studied the crowd, which looked like the normal mix found at carnivals. But there were always a few individuals who stood out—like those guys in front of the beer stand, wearing heavy overcoats. Very strange, considering it was balmy outside. Nick wondered if they were carrying weapons. He'd seen people bring weapons to all kinds of occasions, even carnivals. He relaxed as he watched the suspicious-looking guys saunter toward the exit.

Nick noticed a crowd forming around one of the rides. He smiled suddenly with delight.

"Look." Nick pointed to the wildly curving roller coaster. "That's my—"

"Favorite ride!" Jessica finished for him, grinning up at him. Like little kids, they ran up to where a long line had formed and waited impatiently. The sky was steadily deepening from dark purple to pitch black.

"I hope you're not the queasy type," Nick said, thinking of all the greasy, sugary food they'd just eaten.

"Are you kidding?" Jessica grinned at him. "They don't call me the lead-belly Wakefield for nothing."

Finally they were next in line. Climbing into the rickety seat, Nick held her hand until she was settled behind the safety bar.

As they rattled and bumped through the darkness Jessica whispered in his ear, "If you get scared, you can hold on to me."

Nick chuckled. The ride groaned and squeaked as it picked up speed. Nick and Jessica both rode without holding on, their hands raised over their heads. They were the only ones laughing instead of yelling as they soared and swayed up and down the tracks.

They disembarked into a pleasantly cooling night and began strolling through the grounds.

"Wow, that was great," Jessica breathed. "Oh, look, the ringtoss," she squealed suddenly, tugging at his arm. She pointed to the row of game stalls. "I never win, but I refuse to stop trying."

Nick grinned down at her. "Maybe today will be our lucky day."

Nick couldn't help but notice that Jessica's cheeks were flushed and that her eyes were glowing like stars. He felt his pulse gun a little faster at the same time that he felt a funny tug deep in his heart. His mind knew his reactions weren't from the roller coaster either.

Nick was shaken. Attraction to Jessica was one thing, but he couldn't allow anything more. He was barely aware when Jessica nudged him.

Jessica handed a dollar to the barker and threw Nick a cocky smile. "Aren't you going to watch me win, Nick?"

After Nick had dished out several more dollars, Jessica finally gave up on the ringtoss. Pouting, she tossed her head. "I swear those things are rigged."

"You're probably right," Nick informed her nonchalantly as they walked on. "The mob usually has its hand in running those things. They always set the odds so that they come out ahead. They're in it for the money, after all."

She turned to look at him, surprise in her eyes. "Really? How do you know about that stuff?"

Watch it, Fox, Nick warned himself. One more slip like that and she was bound to get suspicious. "You never heard that? I guess it's just one of those rumors you always hear."

Just then a huge man in a flowered shirt ambled past them, carrying an enormous stuffed giraffe. Wistfully Jessica watched him go by. With an inward sigh of relief Nick changed the subject quickly. "I've always thought that carnivals pay guys like that to carry those things around. I'm convinced no one ever wins them."

"You're probably right," Jessica said dreamily, freeing her hair from its clip. She shook out the flowing golden mane and stretched her arms. Her hair rippled and flowed around her slender body.

Nick swallowed hard and forced his eyes away. Jessica was torturing him. And his willpower was being severely tested. *Remember,* he told himself as he gritted his teeth. *This is strictly business.*

"Hey, Jess, it's the Ferris wheel—we've got to go on that," he said in a deliberately casual tone. He led Jessica to the line in front of the ride's entrance and

83

smiled at her. "It's a dark night filled with stars, perfect for a Ferris wheel ride." The line was moving quickly.

"C'mon," she said eagerly, gazing upward at the huge, glittering wheel. "Let's go." She tucked her hair clip into her purse and grabbed his arm.

In minutes they were fastened into their seats and rising slowly up toward the heavens. The view was spectacular, and the air was cool and tart.

As they reached the top Jessica snuggled closer to him. "I'm a little cold," she said, looking into his eyes. "Too bad I forgot my sweater."

Nick slid his arm around her. "Is that better?" he whispered, pulling her closer until her soft moist lips were only inches from his.

The Ferris wheel suddenly jerked to a stop, letting the people below get on. The jolt did Nick good—though a bucket of cold water would have been better. His brain had overheated and his resolve melted. He was desperately trying to remind himself why he was here. Retreating to his side of the seat, he let his arm drop. *Whew, that was close.*

From the corner of his eye he caught Jessica's disappointed expression but made himself look straight ahead. *Don't cave in,* he coached himself.

You're losing your head, man. This is not a real date. Jessica Wakefield is your dupe, your key to getting into the SVU social scene. Keep telling yourself that over and over. This is strictly business. Sneaking another glance at her delicate profile, he felt himself crumble.

Nick was a drowning man. It would take all his strength not to go under.

"What's going on?" Elizabeth echoed with a weak smile. "I thought we were going out for pizza. You know what pizza is—it's round and made of dough. . . ." She made a circular motion in the air with her hands. "And it's covered with sauce and cheese, and sometimes stuff like pepperoni."

"Very cute," Tom interrupted with a wry look on his face. "Forget the pizza. What I want to know, Elizabeth, is why you stuck a notepad under your pillow." His eyes pinned her, and Elizabeth licked her lips nervously. *Think quickly, Liz, before he gets too suspicious,* she coached herself. She walked to the head of the bed and pulled out the pad.

"I hid this when you came in for a very good reason," she stalled, holding the pad against her chest. "I've written my Christmas presents list on this." Elizabeth reached across to slip the pad under the tower of books that sat on top of her desk. "I decided to start planning my list early."

"Very early, I'd say." Tom arched his suspicious brow. A curious gleam showed in his eyes, and Elizabeth wanted to groan out loud. This surprise party would never fly as long as Tom Watts was around. He was going to weasel all the facts out of her before she even knew it.

She threw him a brilliant smile. "If you shop early, you get the best bargains. This way I won't have to run around like crazy on Christmas Eve."

"I thought you loved shopping on Christmas Eve. You always said that the decorations and the hustle and bustle put you right in the Christmas mood," Tom reminded her.

Elizabeth was tempted for a second to strangle him. She shrugged instead. "I can still go look at the lights and decorations without feeling the pressure of buying gifts at the last minute."

Tom was openly incredulous. "If you say so." A peculiar moment of silence fell between them. "It still seems odd to me. Why not just tell me about your list instead of hiding it? I wouldn't read it without your permission."

Elizabeth shrugged. "I was being silly, I guess. I panicked when I saw you. I just put the pad under my pillow without thinking." She brushed imaginary lint from her pants and straightened her blouse. It was time to get things back on track. "What about our pizza?" she asked brightly. "I'm ravenous. If I wait much longer, I'll collapse from hunger."

Tom stared at her for a long second. "Sure, let's go. Never let it be said that I let a beautiful woman starve."

Following him out the door, Elizabeth almost exhaled loudly with relief. *Well, I got out of that one, but just barely. I'm going to have to avoid Tom until the night of his party. Otherwise the surprise will be blown.* It would be difficult, because Elizabeth wanted to spend every moment she could with Tom. But the sacrifice was worth it. Besides, they'd only be apart for a day and a half. Nothing dramatic could happen in so short a period of time.

Jessica refused to be discouraged. Guys who blew hot and cold usually turned her off, but Nick was so adorable, he was worth figuring out.

The sky was like black velvet draped with diamond-bright stars. It felt good to sit down, even if the Camaro's seats were narrow and low to the ground. Nick rolled down the windows and let the gentle cool air blow in.

Jessica glanced at Nick's handsome profile and wished she could read him better. His abrupt mood shifts baffled her. *But I can handle him,* she decided.

It had been Jessica's idea to leave the carnival. She'd hoped Nick would want to go somewhere private . . . like his place. For a second she wondered if she was being too reckless. But one glimpse of Nick's adorable face from under her lashes convinced her—Jessica definitely wanted to be alone with this guy.

Nick started the car and flashed Jessica a quick smile. "You said something earlier about going somewhere quiet, Jess—isn't there a late-night coffee bar around here? Sinbad's or Simba's, or something like that?"

He drove expertly down the two-lane road, passing several cars and dodging oncoming traffic with ease.

Jessica watched him with admiration. He was smooth and in control, and she liked that. "You're thinking of Sasha's," Jessica offered conversationally. "But let's drive for a while and *then* decide what we want to do." She would think of a way to convince him they should find a more *intimate* setting than a coffee shop.

"Good idea. It's been a long night."

Jessica hoped that didn't mean he was ready to take her home. The night was still young, and she was eager to enjoy it. Jessica stretched her legs and got comfortable.

"Do you mind if I put on the radio?" Jessica asked him.

He shook his head. They had left all the traffic behind, and the road was suddenly deserted. SVU was at least ten miles away. Jessica thought the empty, rural landscape they passed was kind of eerie in the dark. Nothing but stark fields sped by. Jessica didn't see one single house or building.

She fiddled with the radio dial and tried to find a decent station. Opera—yuck. Country—double yuck. And some loudmouthed talk-show host. She frowned as she caught garbled bits of rock and alternative music and a scrap of jazz. Nothing. Darn. *What we need is something romantic or sexy as background music.*

She eyed Nick's glove compartment. *I bet he's got some cool CDs stashed in there.* Nick was the kind of guy who'd have the latest stuff.

She darted a quick look at him. Nick's chiseled face was mysterious, almost aloof in the moonlight pouring through the window.

Jessica shrugged. She was sure he wouldn't mind her looking around for his CDs. She struggled as she pulled on the knob, feeling foolish that she couldn't figure out how to open a glove compartment. Turning the knob left and right didn't work either—maybe she should push in the knob. It clicked.

Nick turned sharply. "Jessica, what are you doing?"

The glove compartment sprang open, and Jessica's heart hurtled to her throat. Her stomach turned into a ball of ice.

Nestled against the stark white of the interior was a black, shining object, its snub nose pointing toward Jessica.

Her throat closed and she couldn't speak. Swiftly Jessica slammed the glove compartment door shut.

But it was too late. She had already seen the gun.

"I don't understand, Alex. Why did you ask me to call you if you don't want to talk?" Noah's voice sounded unnaturally loud through the telephone receiver.

"My head still hurts. And I just told you that I flunked my exam. Doesn't it make sense that I'm in a bad mood?" Alex sounded whiny to her own ears.

"The worst thing you can do is crawl into bed and get depressed. You need to get your endorphins pumping, Alex. Why don't we go running? Or maybe we could go swimming."

"Thanks, but no thanks," Alex said, exhaling deeply. "Exercise isn't going to solve my problems."

Noah was silent for a moment. Alex wound the phone cord around her finger and tapped her foot.

"I have an idea." Noah sounded pleased with himself. "I bet your professor will let you take your exam again if you explain that you suffer from test anxiety."

"I doubt it." Alex sounded sharper than she intended. "He teaches Western philosophy, not psychology. He probably doesn't give a damn about my anxieties."

Noah sighed deeply. "Alex," he said patiently. "What do you want from me? I'm only trying to help."

Alex was instantly contrite. "I'm sorry, Noah, really. I'm not myself right now. I should go to bed and sleep off this bad mood." She tried to make her tone cheerier. "Tomorrow night I'll be back to normal, I promise. We'll have a blast at Alison's dinner."

"I hope so. Are you sure you want to be alone? I'll come over if you'll let me."

Alex didn't want to hurt his feelings, but she needed some space. "I wouldn't be the best company—honestly." She gave an uneasy laugh. "I don't want to push you away with my witchy moods."

"You won't," Noah reassured her in a warm voice. "You'll feel better tomorrow, and don't worry about the exam. Everything will work out. Somehow it always does."

"I hope so," Alex said weakly.

"It's all in your attitude, Alex. Just try to be more positive," he said firmly.

Noah sounded cheery as he said good-bye, and Alex felt guilty. She had acted like a shrew, and he didn't deserve it. Noah cared about her, and she shouldn't have taken her frustrations out on him.

Alex brushed her wavy auburn hair and made a decision. She was going to make it up to Noah, starting tomorrow. She stood in front of her bedroom mirror and made a vow to work on her attitude about life in general.

Forty-five minutes later Alex was humming as she changed into a lavender tunic and more comfortable jeans. She had taken a quick shower and was already feeling a little better. Maybe a walk *would* do her good. Too bad her roommate, Trina, wasn't around. Alex would invite her along and apologize for being such a bear lately.

A stroll to the coffee shop is just the tonic I need, she decided. *A latté will cheer me up, and the fresh air will clear my head.*

It was a gorgeous night, clear and glittering with stars. The coffee shop was only a ten-minute walk from her room.

By the time Alex reached the Red Lion Café, she was almost in a good mood. Depression over her exam had evaporated. All her worries about her other classes were also starting to fade. As she opened the door to the café she saw that the place was hopping. Coffee shops were popular with the students. The tables were filled with people, laughing and playing board games as they sipped their coffees and munched on their pastries. Alex recognized some of the faces from her dorm and waved to a couple of her Theta sisters. The smile suddenly melted from her face.

There was one more person she recognized, but he hadn't noticed her yet. Noah was sitting across the room, his profile facing her.

Alex stared daggers at him, but he didn't look her way—because he was too busy smiling at the simpering blonde who was sharing his cozy little table for two. Noah threw back his head and laughed at something the blond girl said.

Alex was frozen to the floor as her heart dropped with a thud. Her eyes felt hot and her nose tickled. Any second now and she was going to burst into tears. Noah, who had pretended that he was eager to be with Alex, hadn't wasted any time in finding a prettier replacement. Noah, who hadn't bothered to ask if *Alex* wanted to go out for coffee. Now she knew why he was so calm and cheerful. He didn't care anymore; Noah had found someone new.

Alex backed toward the door. Was everyone staring at her? Maybe they all knew about Noah and his new girl and were feeling sorry for Alex.

Noah looked up, his jaw dropping in surprise.

His pretty companion gaped at Alex too. "Alex," he called, getting to his feet. "Wait—you don't understand!"

Alex was out the door. She understood only too well. Noah was dumping her.

Jessica could feel Nick staring at her, but she couldn't meet his eyes. Silence hung heavily between them. The air was suddenly thick inside the Camaro.

"What were you looking for, Jess?" Nick finally asked in a strained voice.

Jessica faked a tiny smile. "I was hoping to find some cool music, but you don't have any CDs. As a matter of fact, the compartment door flew open and slammed shut so fast, I didn't have a chance to really check." She licked her lips and folded her hands on her lap. "But actually I'm not in the mood to listen to anything now." She wondered if he believed her story.

"Oh." Nick's eyes were back on the road, and Jessica couldn't read his expression. His thick lashes hid his eyes.

Jessica's pulse surged as she imagined him pulling over and reaching for his gun. Maybe he was a dangerous criminal. Maybe he was a mobster on the lam. Maybe he was plotting to get rid of her.

"I hope you had a good time tonight," Nick said softly, breaking the stillness. He smiled, his teeth white in the darkness. He reached across and caressed her hand. "I know I did." His velvet voice made her tremble. The spot where he touched her hand tingled.

"It was one of the best nights of my life," she answered shakily, hoping he would touch her again. *What are you doing, you idiot? Why don't you just throw yourself at him?* This guy could be hazardous to her health, and she was acting as if it didn't matter. Guns were dangerous, and nobody knew that more than Jessica Wakefield.

A gun had nearly ruined the lives of Jessica's ex-husband, Mike McAllery, and her brother, Steven. Mike had almost been paralyzed for life, and Steven almost had gone to jail. Luckily they'd avoided both disasters, but still . . .

Nick Fox was mega-trouble. He probably had a record. Maybe even the cops were on his trail. Or— Jessica was struck by a sudden hope—maybe he was a James Bond–type government spy. *He wouldn't hurt me,* she reassured herself. On some instinctive level, she trusted him.

"I think we're both a little tired," Nick announced. "Let's save the coffee for another time."

Jessica was disappointed but refused to show it. "Just remember, I like my espresso strong," she retorted saucily.

"I won't forget," he promised. His eyes met hers for a long, charged moment before returning to the road. "I remember everything about you."

Jessica's heart fluttered. "That's good," she said huskily. "I like a man with a good memory."

She was overcome with the desire to touch the hard biceps moving beneath Nick's shirt as he steered the car. She had to squeeze her hands together so she wouldn't run them through his thick, soft-looking hair. Her tiny voice of common sense wouldn't shut up. *You're a fool*, it said. *This guy is trouble. You're definitely going to end up getting hurt.*

Jessica shut out the voice. Nick was so intriguing, a gorgeous man of danger and darkness. She didn't really know him or any of the details of his past. He was suave and confident, but very elusive.

"Here we are," Nick said, interrupting her thoughts. He pulled up to Dickenson Hall and parked. There was a hush over the campus, and the moon and stars seemed brighter and bigger than usual.

Nick opened her car door. "I'll walk you to your room. It's not safe for you to be out here alone."

Jessica took his arm. "You're right," she said, looking up into his eyes as they glittered in the darkness. "You never know what's lurking around in the dark."

"I won't let anything hurt you," he assured her, a slight smile on his lips.

They reached her dorm room quickly—too quickly for Jessica. She still wanted to drag out the evening. But Nick was obviously ready to call it a night.

Jessica traced the 28 on her door. "It's late," she said softly. "It must be after midnight. I bet my sister's in bed." *I'll have to wake Elizabeth up and tell her about Nick.* "It was fun, Nick," she said with a low-key smile.

Jessica wanted him to think she was cool. She had sounded far too eager in the car. She was also dying to let Nick know that he could tell her who he *really* was—whether he was an undercover agent or a gangster. Jessica bit her tongue, though, not wanting him to think she was some pushy, naive kid.

She moistened her lips, feeling suddenly self-conscious. "Thanks for tonight. I love carni—"

Before she could finish, Nick pulled her to him, his warm lips silencing hers. Jessica slipped her arms around him and found herself sinking into his embrace. The kiss was fierce but soft. And he smelled citrusy and yummy. Tonight his face was clean shaven and smooth as she touched him lightly with her fingertips.

The kiss ended, but they stayed in each other's arms. "Jess—" Nick began. His face was serious.

"Yes?" Her eyes eagerly searched his.

"I—" He stopped. His expression changed, and a careless smile spread across his face. "Why don't you go with me to Alison's party tomorrow night?"

That wasn't what he was going to say at first, Jessica thought in frustration. She lowered her lashes demurely, though she was still quivering from his kiss. Soon Nick would have to reveal more about himself. But not now. "I'd love to go. Why don't you call me?"

"I'll definitely do that," he promised, sliding out from her embrace.

Jessica whispered good night and watched as Nick disappeared into the shadows.

Am I crazy to get so involved in this man's life? Elizabeth asked herself as she sipped chilled apple juice. Mr. Conroy was so sweet, after all. He was almost like an uncle or something to her.

It was so early the next morning that the snack bar was practically empty. The sun was up, but the campus was quiet.

Elizabeth waited patiently while Mr. Conroy drank his black coffee. So far he had completely ignored his soggy cherry danish. Watching Mr. Conroy swallow the dark coffee without coughing, she shuddered to herself. The snack bar's coffee was infamous and the butt of many jokes. The bitter black goo was usually used as a last resort for people pulling all-nighters. But Mr. Conroy didn't seem to mind it. He scarcely seemed aware of what he was drinking.

Elizabeth nibbled her bagel and watched as two bleary-eyed students trudged in and sat down. Elizabeth was bursting with curiosity about Mr. Conroy's quest. She felt as if she were in the middle of a television drama.

Finally Mr. Conroy set down his cup and looked expectantly at Elizabeth. Elizabeth set down her glass of apple juice and cleared her throat. "I hope you don't think I'm being nosy when I ask you this, but how do you know your son lives in this area and attends a university here?" She felt embarrassed, but the question had been nagging at her for a while now.

Mr. Conroy smiled wanly and shook his head. "You shouldn't worry about intruding on my personal life, Elizabeth. You're helping me with a very personal problem, and you deserve to hear the whole story." He paused to swallow another mouthful of the bitter brew. He frowned a moment and then began to speak in a low voice. "I'm stalling, because this is so difficult. . . ."

Elizabeth spoke quickly. "If you don't want to—"

"No." He took a deep breath and continued on. "I want to tell it, even though it deeply shames me now to think about what I was like as a young man. You see, twenty-one years ago I was a completely different person. I was married, but I didn't act like it. I was immature and spent my time drinking and chasing after pretty girls. Why my wife put up with me as long as she did, I'll never know." Mr. Conroy met Elizabeth's eyes, his face suffused with self-disgust.

"I was drunk the night Joan—my wife—gave birth to our son. I was out with another woman and we were in a minor car accident that night—you know about drinking and driving. . . . Well, that's how my wife found out everything.

"Joan left me after that, and I agreed not to contact our son till his twenty-first birthday. Joan immediately took back her maiden name, Antoniani. Since then my life has completely changed. I stopped drinking, found a decent job, became a successful contractor, and finally remarried. Sadly, my second wife has died, and I'm raising our son and daughter alone." For the first time all morning Mr. Conroy smiled a genuine smile. "Would you like to see their pictures?"

"I'd love to," Elizabeth said, reaching to take the two photos he'd pulled out of his wallet.

"That's Jake, he's eight—and Mary, she's ten," he told her proudly.

Elizabeth smiled as she looked at the attractive, grinning faces of his children. "They're adorable," she said sincerely.

"And now it's time for them to meet their big brother. I want to atone for my mistakes, Elizabeth, and more important, I desperately want to find the son I've never met. I only hope I can make it up to him. . . ." Mr. Conroy raised his hands helplessly. "I have to try. As you know, I have very few facts to go on. Joan remarried and lives somewhere in California. She wrote me vague updates in a few letters and sent them through my attorney. No return addresses were ever included. It's been a year or so since I've heard anything. All I know is that my son is attending a prestigious California university. SVU is the last one on my list." He raised desperate eyes. "He has to be here."

"I believe he *is* here, and I know we'll find him," Elizabeth said earnestly, blinking back the tears in her eyes. Mr. Conroy's story was so tragic that she longed to make his dream come true. "I've been thinking hard about our options, Mr. Conroy, and I've come up with another source that we can look into. We can check with the Greater Sweet Valley Bank. If your son goes to school here, then he probably has his money there." Elizabeth stopped to take a drink of her juice. Her mouth was dry from tension.

"Greater Sweet Valley Bank is the major bank for students, though my sister and I do business with a small branch from our bank at home. I don't know if they'll help us, but it's definitely worth a try."

Mr. Conroy leaned forward, the coffee cup gripped between his hands. "It's a great plan. And if it doesn't work out, I'm not going to stop." A determined light shone in his eyes. "I won't rest until I find my son."

Chapter Five

"Don't think you can sweet-talk me into giving you money, sugar." The knife-sharp voice slashed across the phone wires.

Celine took a deep breath and silently counted to five. "Granny Boudreaux, I wouldn't ask if I didn't have a good reason. A few measly old dollars will smooth my way back into SVU society. Don't you want to see your granddaughter rubbing elbows with people of her own class?"

"You're a fool, girl," Granny said. "I don't waste my precious dollars on lost causes. You want money for your little old plan, you'll have to work for it or soft-soap someone else." The old woman cackled. "If those society folks up there have a grain of sense, they won't touch you with a ten-foot pole." Granny Boudreaux hung up with a final thud.

Celine slammed down the phone and glared. The old hag. If only she knew some real voodoo spells, she'd put one on that old woman. Granny Boudreaux had no imagination.

Why couldn't Granny see that Celine's plan was beautiful? Sometimes you had to make people feel they owed you before they'd treat you right. Celine planned on playing the Thetas like a violin, with herself calling the tunes.

Her granny should have known that once Celine put her mind to something, nothing would stand in her way. She was determined to rule the roost at SVU, come hell or high water. There were other ways to get money, and Celine wasn't above using them.

Celine lit a cigarette and blew smoke toward the phone. She was disappointed that Granny had turned her down, but as Granny herself always said, *There's more than one way to skin a polecat*. Celine smiled softly. It was time for plan B.

Elizabeth and Mr. Conroy were both tensely silent as they walked up the steps to the stately looking bank. The building was two stories of pale brick and opaque windows. The double doors were enormous and ornately carved. Elizabeth pushed back the sinking sensation in her stomach. *You can't judge by appearances,* she told herself. Just because the bank looked unfriendly didn't mean she and Mr. Conroy wouldn't get any answers.

As they walked up to the line in front of the tellers' windows, their steps muted by the plush maroon carpet, Mr. Conroy whispered to Elizabeth, "I was expecting a butler to greet us at the door."

Elizabeth whispered back, "I know exactly what you mean. And why are we whispering, anyway?"

Mr. Conroy smiled faintly and shrugged. The line took forever to move forward, and Elizabeth was rehearsing what they would say. She smoothed down her skirt and hoped her blouse was tucked in. She tried not to fidget. *Maybe I should have dressed in more businesslike clothes. Establishments like this seem to treat you better if you look professional. . . .*

Finally they reached an open window. Mr. Conroy stepped forward. "I'll talk to them. Maybe they'll be more responsive to a middle-aged guy like me."

Elizabeth smiled nervously in quick understanding and hovered behind him.

She strained to hear what was being said and had started to step closer when Mr. Conroy turned around.

His face was agitated. "They won't tell me anything. They say it's because of client confidentiality, and I understand that. I tried explaining my predicament and even provided them with references and my attorney's number, but . . ." Mr. Conroy walked over to the oversized leather chairs and sat down.

"Why aren't we leaving?" Elizabeth sat down too. The anticipation of getting news, either good or bad, was draining.

Mr. Conroy rubbed his hands together. "The

manager is the only person who can waive the rules. The teller is asking him if he can see us now."

"That sounds promising," Elizabeth said, eager to seem positive. She brushed her bangs from her eyes.

"Let's hope so, but I'm not counting on it," Mr. Conroy said in a sad voice.

Elizabeth crossed her fingers.

A little more than an hour later they were sitting in the overly air-conditioned office of the bank manager, listening to the bad news. Mr. Phelps, who was reed thin with a reddish brush mustache, was unyielding. No, they could not give out that kind of information; it was privileged. They could not even divulge whether an Antoniani banked there. Doing so would go against company policy.

Elizabeth, watching Mr. Conroy's crushed expression, decided that there must be something this prim little man could do for them. "Mr. Phelps," she began in her sweetest voice, smiling and letting her dimple show. "We wouldn't want to break any rules, of course. Is there anything you can do or any suggestions you can make in order to help us?"

The pale man sniffed, his protuberant eyes expressionless. Sitting behind his enormous mahogany desk, he stared fishily at Elizabeth and Mr. Conroy. "I'm not a detective agency, miss. I can only recommend you hire one."

Elizabeth sighed heavily. Jessica would have had him wrapped around her little finger in seconds. Last night was a perfect example—within the span of one day Jessica had met and nabbed a hot new guy. Jessica had a way with men. *Unfortunately I lack her technique*.

She and Mr. Conroy thanked the bank manager, rose from the icy leather chairs, and started for the door.

Suddenly Mr. Phelps called out to them. "Another thing, if you please. I know you were questioning my tellers, and I can assure you none of them would dream of breaking our rules in order to help you." His mustache quivered at the thought.

And with that Elizabeth closed Mr. Phelps's door behind them.

"Everything seems to be against us," Mr. Conroy said in a low voice. "Maybe this is a sign that I should leave well enough alone, but I just can't."

Elizabeth was immediately contrite. "You can't give up yet. I know we'll find him. This bank isn't our only hope." She patted his arm.

Outside, it was almost a relief to escape the arctic air-conditioning of the bank.

"I'm not giving up, Elizabeth. You've been a real help, and I owe you a great deal," Mr. Conroy said firmly. "Why don't I take it from here? You can give me your bank's address and I'll check with them, though it seems like a real long shot."

Elizabeth pulled out a pen and began writing on a sheet of paper. "Maybe you're right. They may react to you better without me along. Confronting two of us may make them uncomfortable." She handed him the paper and slipped the pen back into her purse.

"Can I drop you off on campus?" He was opening the car door.

Elizabeth shook her head. "I'm not far from the library. I've got some ideas I want to look into. There have to be other ways to track down your son. Besides, the walk will do me good."

"Well, I can only thank you a million times over. I don't know what I'd do without you," he said, smiling shyly. He leaned over and gave her a hug.

The embrace went on a little longer than Elizabeth expected, and she found herself automatically taking a step back. Mr. Conroy dropped his arms. Elizabeth felt her face flush. Mr. Conroy must think she was standoffish and strange, especially after the two of them had become so close so quickly.

Eager to make amends, Elizabeth gave him a reassuring look. "We're almost like family now. I want to help in any way I can."

"I'm glad you feel that way," he said earnestly. He seemed almost reluctant to leave. "Meanwhile I'll have to think of some other strategies. There are a few college officials that I haven't contacted. I'll make a pest of myself if I must."

Elizabeth's heart contracted. "Why don't I call you later from the library? Maybe we can meet again. . . . I can give you the latest news."

"I'll look forward to that," Mr. Conroy said, sliding into the car. "I feel good about us, Elizabeth," he called before shutting the door. "You and I are an unbeatable team."

Jessica walked out of her literature class in a daze. People flowed past her as she ambled out into the sunshine. It was a beautiful Friday afternoon. Anticipation for the weekend filled the air. People were flinging Frisbees, in-line skating, and playing catch out on the quad.

Scenes from her date with Nick last night kept replaying in her mind. Just thinking about the way he kissed her—silky soft but wildly hungry—gave her goose bumps. Part of her wanted to hurry back to her room in case Nick was trying to call her, while the other part of her wanted to drink up the sunshine and daydream.

Jessica shifted her notebook under her arm and squeezed past a couple kissing in the middle of the sidewalk. She suddenly came to a dead halt, forcing other people to squeeze around her too. But Jessica was oblivious.

Only ten feet away from her, lounging on the grass, was a shirtless Nick Fox—soaking up some rays. He was stunning. Muscular and lean, Nick looked even better without his shirt than he did with it on. He was busy talking on his cellular phone and didn't seem to notice Jessica standing there.

Jessica grinned wickedly. She would sneak up behind and surprise him. Walking softly toward him, with his back still to her, she heard his voice. That deep, knock-your-socks-off voice she couldn't get enough of.

"It'll all come down in the next two days. I'll pick up the delivery, and then we'll make our move. No. Nobody suspects a thing."

Jessica felt a delicious thrill run up her spine. She was right! Nick *was* a government spy, picking up top-secret documents or something equally important.

Nick hung up. *Now's my chance to surprise him,* Jessica thought, trembling slightly with nerves. She tiptoed up behind him and slipped her hands over his eyes. "Guess—"

Before she could finish her sentence, she was grabbed by her arm and flipped to the ground. In a flash Nick straddled her, his hands around her throat. He was breathing quickly, and his eyes were savage. Jessica was pinned to the ground and helpless. Nick the nice guy was gone, replaced by Nick the dangerous mystery man.

Panting, he stared in horror down at her. "Jessica!" he shouted. "Don't ever do that again. I could have killed you!"

Aha! she thought. Even though her heart was pounding, she couldn't keep a triumphant smile off her face. Jessica had hoped Nick might overreact, especially after she'd seen him grab Celine. And now that he had, Nick would be forced to give the *real* reason he was so aggressive . . . always on edge. She certainly didn't buy the story he gave Celine.

She gazed up at him. "What a way to greet a girl! I don't think I've ever been tossed around like that before." Her blue-green eyes shone with open curiosity as he released her and moved to sit beside her on the grass.

Nick just shook his head.

Jessica sat up and picked the leaves from her hair. Slowly licking her lips, she said, "I'm pretty shaken up. What are you going to do to make it all better?"

"He's got to be listed somewhere. I just have to find him," Elizabeth said, thinking out loud.

"If you're looking for Tom, he's probably over at WSVU."

The familiar voice made Elizabeth spin around. She broke into a big smile. "Nina, hi. I was talking to myself and didn't even see you."

Nina grinned. "Obviously. You were lost in another world. So what's going on? Surely you haven't really lost Tom."

Elizabeth laughed and shook her head. A few people looked up and shushed them, so she mimed to Nina that she should follow her into an empty study room. The library was packed with serious-looking students huddled over books and pads, and Elizabeth didn't want to disturb them more. She *did* want to talk to Nina Harper, her dearest friend at SVU.

Nina was levelheaded, very bright, and good-hearted. Nina and Elizabeth had been through thick and thin together—literally. In the beginning of their freshman year both girls had put on a few extra pounds and had turned to each other for support. Becoming diet buddies had not only helped them lose weight but had also cemented their friendship. Just seeing Nina always made Elizabeth feel better.

They walked into a study room and plopped down into the nearest folding chairs. Nina groaned and rolled her shoulders, sending her beaded braids clicking.

"I've been beating my brains out for my upcoming physics exam. I keep seeing random equations floating in front of my eyes. I also have a bio report due next week."

"You have my sympathy," Elizabeth said sincerely.

"I just keep telling myself that this will all pay off someday." Nina grinned. "The problem is my brain keeps begging me for a payoff now."

"There's always hunky Bryan as your reward," Elizabeth said, nudging Nina and waving her eyebrows à la Groucho Marx. Bryan Nelson was a real catch. Handsome, dedicated, and intelligent, he was the president of the Black Student Union, and he was all Nina's. Even though they were in many ways opposites—Nina was a scientist, an athlete, and not very political, and Bryan was a serious activist who had little time for sports or anything else—they were madly in love.

Nina half shut her eyes and smiled dreamily. "He

certainly is a treat. Hunky, smart, and serious." Nina opened her eyes. "Sometimes he's so serious he's a little grim, actually."

"Speaking of grim, Tom has been in a really grumpy mood lately." Elizabeth frowned and shifted in her seat.

"Tom? What's wrong with him?" Nina piled her books on a nearby chair and stifled a yawn.

Elizabeth sighed, brushing a loose strand of golden hair from her mouth. She tucked the wisp back into her ponytail. "He hasn't said much. Just that he's depressed that his family won't be able to celebrate his birthday with him tomorrow."

Nina's wide dark eyes softened with compassion. "It's so sad that he lost his entire family. As much as they drive me crazy, I can't imagine life without my parents."

"I know what you mean," Elizabeth said. "That's why I'm throwing this surprise party. It will do him a world of good. While his friends can't replace his family, at least Tom will know that they all care about him. I hope the love and affection floating around the party will ease some of his depression."

"I think it's just the thing he needs," Nina said firmly. "I remember how I felt after Bryan and I were attacked by the secret society. Nothing made me heal faster than having my friends around." Nina suddenly swooped up her purse. "I'm trying to fight off hunger pangs." She held out a roll of sugar-free mints. "Want one?"

"Yeah, thanks." Elizabeth popped the mint into her mouth. "I don't know how long I'll be in here. I probably won't have time for a real meal, so your mint just may be dinner."

Nina smiled at her, curiosity in her eyes. "I don't want to be nosy, but why are you spending such a beautiful day locked in this stuffy library? Do you have a major paper to do or something?"

Elizabeth's sea-colored eyes widened, and she pulled her chair closer. Eagerly she began relaying the whole Mr. Conroy tale to Nina, who made sympathetic noises and shook her head in disbelief.

"You can imagine how desperate Mr. Conroy is to find his son. He really wants to make amends. I can tell that he loves his son very much, even though he's never met him."

"That's a fantastic story. If anyone can help Mr. Conroy, I know you can, Liz," Nina said with assurance.

"Thanks for the vote of confidence. So far I've been batting zero." Elizabeth shrugged. "But the fight's not over yet."

"Speaking of fights." Nina cocked her head thoughtfully to one side. "Did you really invite Todd to Tom's party?"

Elizabeth nodded. "I know they're not exactly friends, but they are civil. I thought the party would be good for Todd too. He's really changed. He wants to make up for the past and prove that he can really succeed. Todd can use all the support he can get.

He's all alone now. . . ." Elizabeth hurriedly filled Nina in on Todd's reinstatement with the basketball team and his separation with Gin-Yung.

"Wow, things really change fast when you're not looking." Nina shook her head. Her dark-beaded braids bounced against her cheek. Nina grabbed one of the braids and frowned down at it. "Change— that's what I need. Take the braids, for instance. I'm getting pretty sick of this look. It's way too childish. I dare you to tell me I don't look like I should be carrying a lunch box and a teddy bear."

Elizabeth chuckled and studied her friend's face. Nina's smooth brown-skinned, round-cheeked face was very pretty. The braids did enhance her youth- fulness, but Elizabeth didn't see anything wrong with that. After all, Elizabeth herself frequently wore her own hair in a ponytail. Nina looked serious about this, though, and Elizabeth would support her quest for a new image.

"I think you look very attractive, but a new hair- style is always fun. What are you going to do?" Elizabeth asked, trying to picture Nina without her braids.

"I'm not sure. Did you ever see Arla Reed's hair? You know her, she's in *City Heat*. She wears it chin length and curly, and sort of asymmetrical. I just saw pictures from her wedding to her on-screen boyfriend, and she looked so beautiful."

"Hmmm." Elizabeth gazed at Nina, tapping her chin with her finger. "Could be a winner, Nina."

Suddenly Elizabeth snapped upright. "Weddings—that's it!" She leaned over to hug Nina. "You're a genius, girl. I'm going to search wedding announcements and look for an Antoniani. Mr. Conroy said his ex remarried, and the announcements would list Mrs. Antoniani's groom's last name. That could be his son's new last name." Elizabeth was so excited, she could scarcely wait to get started. "You're the greatest, Nina!"

Nina laughed good-naturedly. "Thanks, but I didn't do anything. I just rambled on about my hair. I'm glad I could help."

Elizabeth pulled out a pen and began jotting down notes on her pad. "It's amazing, Nina. I never know where I'll get my next inspiration." Her eyes sparkled. "I was just about to give up hope. Maybe you should stick around. Who knows what other ideas you'll come up with?" Elizabeth was bursting with new energy.

Nina smiled and stood up. As she watched Elizabeth bounce in her seat, she teased, "You better get to the microfilm section before you explode. And I have get back to physics."

As they headed out the door Nina paused with a solemn expression on her face. "I hope you find the son, Elizabeth. I really do."

Nick pulled Jessica against his chest. She felt the wild beating of his heart seconds before he kissed her. Nick moved closer, his face mere inches from her own. The savage look slowly melted from his face as he kissed her once, twice, three passionate times. The intensity built with each kiss. Their lips couldn't get enough of each other, and Jessica's heart soared.

Nick buried his fingers into her long blond hair and murmured her name. "Jess."

Jessica slid her arms around him, enjoying the hard strength of his muscled back. The fresh scent of the grass beneath them mingling with Nick's musky cologne made Jessica feel almost faint. And Nick seemed to be finding breathing as difficult as she was. She forgot they were sitting on the quad. Actually she forgot about the entire campus—the world had rapidly faded away. And Jessica had melted into a pool of deep, warm emotions.

Abruptly Nick released her. He sighed hugely and ran his hands over his dark hair. "We better cool it, Jess. Unless you like an audience." With an arched brow he nodded toward the streams of passersby. Students were pouring out of the surrounding buildings.

Jessica felt her face heat up. She nodded and smoothed her hair, finger combing the long, silky strands. As she watched him tug his shirt on, she decided it was time for her to get some answers.

"OK, Mr. Fox, it's time to fess up," she demanded lightly. She drew her knees up against her chest and cocked her head. "What are you really doing here at Sweet Valley University?"

"Doing?" He faced her, tucking his small cellular phone into his jeans pocket. "I'm trying to get an education, just like you."

"Right. You really don't expect me to believe that, do you?" she asked sarcastically. "And should I also believe that all students carry around cellular phones?" Jessica added with a devilish smile.

"Well, this one does."

"OK. But all students do *not* carry guns," Jessica challenged.

"I was afraid you'd seen that last night," Nick said ruefully. "It's legit. I carry it for protection. I was robbed in L.A. not long ago and immediately got myself a permit. In my neighborhood most people are packing heat these days."

Jessica frowned thoughtfully and plucked a blade of grass. It sounded reasonable, but her intuition told her that Nick was lying. After all, why would Nick need to carry a gun in his car now that he was at Sweet Valley University? Plus his explanation was a little too slick. She wound the blade around her finger. "It just doesn't add up, Nick. You're far from being like any regular student I've ever met."

Nick's face hardened. "If you don't believe me, Jess, then how can we be friends? I don't hang out with people who don't trust me."

Jessica heard an insistent chirping sound. Before she could respond, Nick was pulling out a beeper. He briefly studied the display screen before turning it off and shoving it back into his pocket.

Nick met her eyes with a weak smile. "I know what you're going to ask, but I carry a beeper because I'm looking for work. This way prospective employers can always track me down. I don't have an answering machine and can't afford to miss important calls."

Jessica's blue-green eyes were sizzling with questions. But before she could ask them, Nick was leaning forward for a quick kiss. With catlike grace he leapt easily to his feet. Holding out his hand, he pulled her upright.

"So," he said, gathering her closer. "What's it going to be? Do you trust me?"

Jessica nodded, mesmerized by his piercing green eyes. *I trust you to tell me the truth someday*, she amended to herself.

"If only you weren't so *mysterious* about yourself, Nick," she murmured, her lips barely inches from his.

"I told you . . . I'm a boring subject—too boring to waste time talking about," he whispered huskily. "I've got to run, but how about one more for the road?" Deftly he tilted her chin up for one more quick but luscious kiss.

Jessica felt the earth wobble as he released her. She wanted to tell him his excuse for carrying a beeper was pretty weak—that all his excuses were—but her lips wouldn't move. She could only gaze at him giddily.

He brushed his fingers tenderly against her cheek.

"I'll pick you up tonight at seven for Alison's party. See you then, Jess."

After he'd left, Jessica walked slowly back home. Nick was the most intriguing man she'd ever met, and the most frustrating. She'd get to the bottom of Nick's mysteries. He didn't know how determined and crafty Jessica could be.

I won't stop till I've figured you out, Nick Fox. . . .

Chapter Six

"Tom—Tom Watts. *W-a-t-t-s*." Tom stared at the phone in disbelief.

"Do you work here at WSVU?" the chirpy voice on the other end of the line replied.

"Well, yes. I'm the station manager. And who did you say you were?" His voice was a growl.

"Oops." The girl giggled nervously. "I'm the new trainee. I guess we've never met. I just started today part-time."

"Great," Tom said in a voice thick with sarcasm. "Can you check around and tell me if Elizabeth Wakefield is there now? She's a reporter." He rolled his eyes to the heavens and tapped his fingers on his desk. As he waited he met Danny Wyatt's eyes. His roommate was sitting at his desk, studying.

Danny grinned at him. "Hard day?"

Tom nodded glumly. "Hard week."

The girl came back on the line. "Sorry, but

there's no Elizabeth here. Is there anything I can do?" she offered helpfully.

"I doubt it," Tom said brusquely. He hung up forcefully.

Danny arched his brows.

Tom rubbed his eyes and groaned. "I know I sounded like a grouch, but"—he picked the phone back up and began punching buttons—"I can't find Liz. I already tried her room. Maybe she's at Nina's."

He scowled as the phone rang eight times with no answer. Sighing, he hung up and sank down onto his bed. "Where is she? Elizabeth is always at WSVU this time of the day. I know she doesn't have classes. I've got her schedule memorized as well as my own."

Danny closed his book and spun around on his seat. "What's the deal, Tombo? It's not like you to be so uptight. Why are you so worried about Elizabeth?"

Tom sighed, feeling foolish. Danny was one of the few people he opened up to, but he still felt silly burdening him with his worries. Danny was a good guy, a steady friend with the kind of humorous outlook that always cheered Tom up. Tom and Danny were both private and independent, but they gave each other support when needed.

"Elizabeth has been acting weird these last few days. I can't help but feel that she's avoiding me."

"Are you sure you're not blowing things out of proportion? Maybe she's caught up with a new story or something."

"Yeah." Tom ran his fingers through his hair. "You're probably right. I know she stumbled across some story while she was talking to the bursar the other day. But she didn't give me any details."

"Maybe she's waiting till she uncovers more facts. You journalists are a closemouthed lot when it comes to your stories."

"It's not just that," Tom said slowly, struggling for the words. He thought about when Elizabeth hid her notepad, but decided it was too silly to bring up. "She seems distracted. Even when we're talking, I feel like her mind's on other things."

Danny shook his head. He got up and began pulling on cream-colored sweats, the light material contrasting sharply with the rich brown of his skin. "I've got to be honest, Tombo. It doesn't sound that serious to me. Maybe you just need some perspective. Why don't you and I go down to the gym and do some reps? It'll take your mind off everything." He tucked shoes into his bag and pulled a towel from the closet.

"I don't know. Something's going on with Elizabeth—I can feel it," Tom said with a frown. "I just wish she'd come clean with me and tell me what's up." He picked up a framed recent photo of himself and Elizabeth from his desk. Her beautiful face backlit by sunlight gazed up at him with affection in the picture. They looked like a couple in love. He set the photo back down. Had something happened to change the way Elizabeth felt about him since that picture was taken a few weeks ago?

Danny snapped him lightly with a towel. "Come on, man," he said with an infectious grin. "Let's go work up some sweat. Give your brain a rest."

"Not that I've been using it for studying." Tom got to his feet. He cast a rueful look at the stack of homework on his desk. "I guess the family tree for my sociology class can wait. I haven't accomplished anything today anyway. Maybe a good workout will clear my head."

"That's the spirit," Danny said cheerily, watching as Tom began stuffing his own gym bag.

As they headed for the door Tom stopped in his tracks. "If Liz is hiding something from me, I'm going to find it out." He pulled out his keys, ready to lock the door behind them. "You know me, Danny. I won't stop until I uncover the truth."

Grinning brides and grooms in black and white whirled in front of Elizabeth until they all blurred into one. Elizabeth couldn't believe how many people had gotten married over the years, and they'd all announced their nuptials in the newspapers! For a moment Elizabeth was dazzled by a dreamlike image of Tom and her announcing their wedding in the paper, she in a floating white gown, Tom in a tux. . . .

Elizabeth gave herself a shake and returned to the screen in front of her. She had been sitting in the library for hours, only taking a couple of quick breaks to grab snacks from the vending machine in the lounge. Groaning out loud, she wished the system was on a computer database so she could search more efficiently. This way she had to visually scan all the newspaper wedding announcements by hand on the microfilm machine.

There must be a quicker way to find Joan Antoniani's wedding announcement, Elizabeth thought. *Maybe if I just skim through quickly and only pay attention to names that begin with the letter* A, *it might be faster.* Elizabeth turned the machine's knob and tried her technique. Unfortunately there were dozens of Adams, Allens, and Andersons, but not a single Antoniani. Her head felt as if there were a tiny person inside, pounding nails into it. And her eyes were raw from staring at the microfilm.

Elizabeth sighed. Once she started a job, she had to finish it. That was just her way. And she still had lots of film to search. With a shrug she went back to work.

Approximately one hour later Elizabeth was finished. Collecting the microfilms, she returned them to the cabinet with a heavy heart. There hadn't been a single Antoniani in the entire stack. She'd have to give poor Mr. Conroy bad news again. Dragging her heels, she made her way to the bank of pay phones at the library entrance.

Elizabeth dialed the Sunny Ridge Inn, and Mr. Conroy picked up on the first ring. He must have been waiting for the call, Elizabeth thought worriedly.

They exchanged hellos quickly, and Elizabeth got right to the heart of the matter.

"I'm so sorry, but I didn't find anything," she said, her tone heartfelt.

"Don't feel bad, Elizabeth. I didn't either. The other bank was a washout, and none of my university contacts panned out. To be honest, most of my contacts didn't seem very motivated. One of them, though, a Ms. Zucco, who works with SVU's vice president, really did try to find any data on my son. But she also turned up nothing." Mr. Conroy sounded deeply depressed. "I even called the Department of Motor Vehicles, but that was a dead end too." He paused for a second. "I don't want to give up, though. I hope you don't either." Mr. Conroy's tone was pleading.

"I'm not throwing in the towel yet," Elizabeth reassured him firmly. "I think we should meet again tomorrow and plot out our next step."

Mr. Conroy sounded much more cheery when he said good-bye.

Washing her face with cool water in the rest room, Elizabeth began to feel a little better. Pictures of beaming brides and grooms would probably stay in her mind for hours. *Which reminds me, I haven't spoken to Tom all day.* Elizabeth missed him. But she knew she had to stay away from him until Saturday night. How else could she keep his party a secret? Yawning and rubbing her eyes, Elizabeth nearly staggered outside into the dusk. She'd call him when she got home. Tom probably hadn't even noticed her absence.

"I'm just going to have to show up at Alison's naked!" Jessica screamed as she stared in her closet with dismay. She had absolutely nothing to wear to Alison's formal dinner tonight. Running her hand through her hangers, she wrinkled her nose. This was pitiful; not one of her outfits was remotely right for the party or for wowing Nick. She took a peek at Elizabeth's clothes, neatly pressed and hanging in a tidy row, and shook her head. She knew she was desperate if she even considered her sister's stuff. Elizabeth's specialty was plain and conservative. There wasn't a glittery or slinky item in her entire wardrobe. Elizabeth didn't own a single piece of clothing that Jessica would be caught dead in.

If I were Lila, I would run down to the Like Wow Boutique and buy something new. Unfortunately Jessica's bank account was quite a bit smaller than Lila's. Gloomily she pulled out a blue satin bustier, jacket, and skirt before discarding it.

"Too flashy," she said to no one in particular. She could just see Alison's sneer if she wore that. Her black backless was too plain.

"Here we go. Pure perfection." She brought out her pale pink velvet sheath. It fit perfectly and was seductive without going overboard. Matching heels would complete the look. Jessica swirled her hair up on top of her head with one hand and held the dress in front of her with the other. She smiled into the mirror. The pink tones of the dress made her skin even more golden and showed off her slender shape. With her willowy five-foot, six-inch build, she could carry off most fashions. So could Elizabeth, but of course Elizabeth never deviated from her boring wardrobe. Jessica would put her hair up in a chignon, making her look older, more cosmopolitan. Nick would go crazy when he saw her in that dress.

There was a knock on the door. Jessica shoved aside the clothes heaped on her bed and jumped to get it.

Lila stood there, chic as usual, with curiosity written all over her face. She glided through the door and took in the explosion on Jessica's bed.

"Getting ready for tonight?" She settled herself onto Elizabeth's spotless bed. "I thought I'd drop by and see if you needed any help." She ran long, manicured nails through her silky brown hair and crossed her legs. She was wearing black jeans and a matching silk top.

Jessica grabbed up the sheath and swished it under Lila's nose. "Isn't this perfect, Li? Picture me wearing these shoes and my hair up like this." Her blue-green eyes were bright and expectant as she pulled her hair off her face.

Lila nodded. "It's perfect. I've got to hand it to you, Jess. You'll have just the right look—sexy and sophisticated."

Jessica dropped to her bed, clutching the sheath. She ignored the clothes tangled underneath her. "I suppose you've got something picked out that will make me and everyone else look pathetic," she said dramatically. It was hard to beat Lila, with her fortune and her fashion sense.

Lila preened. "You should see the dress I found at Evita's, that new boutique downtown."

Jessica felt a swell of jealousy. Evita's was exclusive and very expensive. The clothes displayed in the window were gorgeous.

"It's a black-and-white silk strapless, with a matching stole. Very proper until I take the stole off. . . ." A wicked grin flashed across Lila's face. "I can't wait until Bruce sees it. He'll simply die."

Jessica shook her head. "Bruce and all the guys at the party—"

"Speaking of men," Lila interrupted her smoothly. "May I assume that you're wearing that dress purely to impress that hot new guy you went out with last night?"

Jessica blushed, thinking about what had happened with Nick earlier on the quad.

Lila narrowed her eyes. "Tell me everything. If he's got you so worked up, this new guy must be something."

"Words can't describe it, Lila. Nick is a totally exciting guy, much more worldly than the *boys* we usually date. I think I know why too. He lives on the edge. You won't believe what I found in his glove compartment," Jessica breathed eagerly, and proceeded to tell about the gun, the overheard telephone conversation, and the beeper.

There was a long silence while Lila stared at Jessica. Finally Lila spoke. "You better watch this guy closely, Jessica. Your Nick Fox sounds more like a drug dealer than a spy to me."

"A drug dealer!" Jessica squealed. "Don't be ridiculous. He wouldn't be into anything like that. I know him, Lila, and I'm convinced that he's a government spy. He's too smooth and good looking to be into drugs."

"Do you think you have to pass an ugly test before they let you sell drugs? Honestly, Jessica, if you saw some of the tough guys Tisiano and I ran across in his computer business, you would swear they were models for some Italian fashion magazine. I think you should tell Nick tonight that you can't see him anymore. This guy sounds too dangerous."

Jessica gaped at her in amazement. Sometimes Lila was so surprisingly melodramatic.

"Don't worry about me, Lila. I know what I'm doing. And I can handle myself."

Tom threw down his pen and kicked it hard across the room. Watching it bounce against the wall and drop into the wastebasket, he clapped in mock applause. *He shoots . . . he scores!* He slammed his notebook shut and rubbed his brow wearily. He'd spent all afternoon hunched over the family tree assignment, and he hadn't even completed it yet.

Outside, the sun was down and the sky was

black. Tom was tired and hungry. "Hey, maybe I can catch Liz before she heads out to dinner," he said to himself, rubbing his flat stomach. "Maybe she'll give me a break and eat with me." Chastising himself for being a grouch, he waited while the phone rang and rang.

After five rings a sleepy voice croaked, "Hello?"

Tom was surprised and a little worried. "Elizabeth, is that you? Are you sick?"

She cleared her throat. "No, just really, really tired."

Tom sighed. "Where've you been? I've been looking for you all day."

She yawned deeply over the phone. "Can we talk about it later? I'm so exhausted I can barely think. I'm sorry I didn't call. I meant to, but I lost track of time."

I guess I'm not all that important to her anymore, Tom thought. Out loud he said, "That's fine. I was a little worried when I didn't hear from you."

"I'm doubly sorry. Is that why you called—because you were worried?" She yawned again.

"No, I was hungry and hoping you might be too. But I can tell you're too tired to go out. Go back to sleep, Elizabeth. I'll call you tomorrow." He hung up and sat down on the bed. Tomorrow was his twenty-first birthday, and he was all alone. And hungry. A sardonic smile twitched his lips. There was that self-pity again.

"Hey, Watts—why are you sitting in the dark?" Danny's cheerful voice stirred him from his sad thoughts. Tom gazed around in surprise. With night falling outside, his small desk lamp barely illuminated their dark room. Danny switched on the overhead light, flooding the room in brightness. Then he clapped Tom on the back. "I thought you might be here. If you're as hungry as I am, I've got a great Cajun place we can try."

"Danny, my man, you are a lifesaver. I was about to collapse with hunger." Tom grinned up at his roommate and felt his mood instantly brighten. "All those reps down in the weight room must have used up a million calories."

"I know. All through my last class my stomach was growling like crazy."

"I asked Liz if she wanted to go out, but she was too tired. . . ." Tom tried to hold his smile but failed.

"I don't mind playing second fiddle to Elizabeth," Danny said, taking his wallet from his pocket.

Tom studied Danny for a puzzled moment; then he snapped his fingers. "Hey, weren't you supposed to be at that dinner with Isabella tonight? You didn't forget, did you? Isabella will kill you."

Danny nodded as he checked inside the wallet before sliding it back into his pocket. "I didn't forget," he said casually. "Izzy and I talked, and I explained I wasn't up to some highfalutin affair catered by Alison Quinn. Somehow I couldn't picture our resident snob smiling across the table at me—probably the only guy who isn't on her daddy's payroll." He lifted one shoulder, his face a picture of nonchalance. "Isabella understood."

Tom gave him a suspicious look. Danny and Isabella were a deeply committed couple. He couldn't believe that Danny, who was a strong, self-confident person, would let an idiot like Alison Quinn stop him from escorting Isabella to the dinner. Danny's face was a picture of innocence. Too much so.

He's here because of me, Tom realized. Danny was a real pal. Tom knew he should send him back to Isabella and their party. But he really needed Danny's company tonight. *I'm allowed to be selfish for once.* And with that he followed Danny out the door.

"Where did you say we're going?"

"Cajun Corners—it's a new place off the boulevard." Danny looked dreamy eyed with anticipation. "Then we should head over to this bar I know. They have seventy-five-cent pitchers. Of course, this place has little—shall we say—ambiance." Danny's eyes gleamed as he watched the slow smile spread across Tom's face. "C'mon, Tom, don't forget in just a few short hours, you'll be a legal adult. Time to celebrate, buddy. I'll even spring for a cab so we don't have to worry about getting home later tonight."

Tom reached across to slap his palm against Danny's. "All right, I'm ready, Mr. Wyatt. I can hardly wait to see this dive—er—I mean, pub."

Danny winked at him. "You were right the first time, and if we hurry, we can still make it in time for the fifty-cent shots at happy hour!"

"Adulthood, here I come!"

Chapter Seven

"Alex, you have to believe me. I'm not cheating on you." Noah's voice sounded annoyed over the phone. "Phoebe is just a girl in my behavioral psych lab. I was in the mood for some caffeine and went to the Red Lion, and *she* came over and sat with me. She had some questions about our lab," Noah said wearily.

"Right." Alex sulked. She knew she wasn't being fair. This was the third time Noah had called since she saw him with that girl the night before. He had explained each time about Phoebe, the blonde in the coffee shop. Noah had wanted to come over last night and this morning, but Alex had told him no. It was Friday and she had skipped all her classes. She couldn't even make herself get out of bed.

Alex sensed Noah was telling her the truth about Phoebe, but she couldn't stop herself from being grouchy and suspicious. She brushed cookie crumbs from her bedspread and crumpled up the empty cookie bag. She had just demolished its entire contents.

Noah sighed loudly after the long silence. "Am I still invited to Alison's dinner tonight? Or am I banished forever?"

Give Noah a break. He's a great guy and doesn't deserve this, Alex told herself. She tossed the bag at the wastebasket and made a face as it missed and bounced on the floor. *Swallow your pride and tell him you're sorry.*

Alex brushed her hair from her face and took a deep breath. "Of course I want you to come. I can't face Alison's surprise announcement without you," she halfheartedly teased. "I'm sorry, Noah. I know you told the truth about Phoebe." Alex had to get a grip on herself. Did she want to drive Noah away?

"Listen, Alex, I know why you were so upset. I would have been a little angry if I saw you having coffee with another guy. It's no big deal—let's just put it behind us."

Noah sounded sympathetic, and Alex felt immediately guilty. She squirmed, disgusted with herself. She pulled the blankets around her and glanced down at her unmade bed. The covers were all tangled up with the crumpled clothes she wore yesterday. Her side of the room was looking pretty messy, and Alex was surprised Trina hadn't complained yet.

"OK. Now we can have a really good time tonight." Alex crossed her fingers. Maybe tonight would be so much fun that she'd pull herself out of this mood.

"That sounds great to me," he said warmly. "We could both use a few laughs."

Alex smiled shakily. "You know, I feel better already. I have a feeling that tonight's going to be one of those nights we'll never forget."

Don't fall apart, Fox, Nick warned himself. *Stick to your agenda. Fight the temptation.* Beautiful women always had a disconcerting effect on him, and Jessica Wakefield packed a double whammy.

Jessica daintily crossed her ankles, showing her long, sleek, tanned legs. As Nick's eyes traveled upward he gulped silently. The rest of her looked just as good, if not better. He'd never seen the nape of her neck before, and with her hair up it made a tempting target for his lips. Startled, he suddenly realized that he was almost on top of the car in front of him. Nick tapped the brakes and swore to himself.

"This is such a cool car, Nick," Jessica said, patting the seat. "Have you had it long?"

Nick shifted uneasily. He couldn't tell her the truth. "Yeah, for a while now," he answered vaguely.

She gave him an exasperated look, but then smiled at him. "I like your suit, Nick," Jessica said sweetly. "You look so natural in it. Many men don't seem to get the fit right." She brushed a stray wisp of hair from her mouth and tucked it back into her chignon. "They either look like old sacks or sausages bursting out of their skins. You look perfect." She touched the fabric on his arm with an appreciative smile.

He darted her a quick smile. "I'm not usually a suit-and-tie kind of guy, but I made an exception for tonight." *This suit better look good after I spent all that money on it.* Nick had gone a little crazy at that expensive men's shop.

"Nick." She examined him through her long lashes, dimple flashing in her smooth cheek. "I was just wondering. I mean, I don't want to pry. . . . But I want to know more about you."

Nick swiveled his eyes back to the road and kept his hands steady on the steering wheel. The guy driving the big sedan in front of him kept hitting his brakes. It was making him tense. Maybe it was intentional—if only he could get a glimpse of the driver. . . .

"Nick, are you listening?" Jessica sounded plaintive.

"I wish I had something exciting to tell you, Jess. But I've led a pretty ordinary life."

"Then why won't you tell me more, like did you have a serious girlfriend at your old school? And have you ever used that gun in your glove compartment?" Jessica watched him alertly.

Nick laughed shortly. "What do you think, Jess?" He glanced at her from the corner of his eye.

"C'mon, Nick. Don't be so mysterious."

"Jessica, Jessica," he teased. "Haven't you ever heard about what happened to the curious cat?"

She pretended to pout. "You're mean. I'll tell you about my life. Just ask me something—anything."

"And I want to hear every last detail." He couldn't resist her and reached over to squeeze her hand. "I promise I'll tell you my whole story someday. You just need to be patient. Think you can wait?" He gazed for a second into her eyes, losing himself in their blue-green depths. *Don't keep asking,* he pleaded silently. *I'm likely to cave in at any minute, and then we'd both be in danger.*

She nodded. "Normally I'm not a patient person, but for you I'll make an exception."

"Why don't you tell me about this party we're going to?" Nick suggested. The sedan was slowing down again. Was the driver staring at Nick from his rearview mirror? Nick's muscles relaxed as the sedan suddenly turned right at the next intersection. He sent Jessica a quick smile. "Is it some boring and uptight affair, or do you think there might be a little excitement?"

Jessica slanted him a look. "Excitement—at Alison Quinn's dinner? It depends on what you call exciting. Alison's been building up this big surprise announcement that she's going to make, but I doubt it will be anything much."

Even in the dark with the only light coming from the moon, Jessica's beauty seemed to glow—her delicately tanned skin, her golden hair, her shining eyes, everything. Distracted, Nick forced his attention back to business.

"I was wondering," he said carefully. "Do people at sorority parties get wild—you know, drink or do drugs? Where I went to school before, lots of kids were into cocaine and pot. It was pretty common to see people using at clubs and parties."

Jessica wrinkled her nose. "Yuck, you must have known some pretty major losers, Nick." She gave him a funny look. "Were they friends of yours?"

Nick shrugged. "No, I just knew them. I guess you're not into the drug scene, huh?"

"No way. Who would want to mess up their lives with drugs?" She shook her head in disbelief. "You'd have to be crazy!"

There goes my plan to use Jessica. Right down the drain. She obviously can't help me meet the right people. Nick bit his lip in frustration and then sighed softly. But he was glad she was straight. The drug business could get pretty rough. At least he wouldn't drag her into the thick of it. Mixing business and pleasure never worked.

Nick could feel Jessica's inquisitive stare. He gave her a reassuring smile and watched as she pulled down the vanity mirror to check her hair. Jessica didn't have a clue about what was going on in the world—that there were lots of people eager to use and sell all kinds of drugs.

He frowned to himself. His relief that Jessica

wasn't part of the scene worried him. He was getting too involved; he was losing his distance. This was the kind of situation that could get him into trouble, and he should have known better. He was a professional.

After all, if Jessica wasn't a genuine connection, then he had no excuse for hanging around her. None that made sense, at least.

"Well, one thing I can guarantee is the food. Alison has the best caterer in town at her disposal," Jessica interrupted his thoughts. She tossed her head with a mischievous smile. "And we can always leave if we get bored."

"If I may have your attention, please. This announcement will affect every Theta." Alison smiled excitedly and let her gaze sweep around the room. She stood at the head of her table and tapped on her crystal goblet with a spoon. "Over the last few days I've been hinting about a wonderful surprise. I know you're all *very* curious." She stopped, coughed, and held up her hand in apology as she lifted her glass of water for a quick sip.

Jessica rolled her eyes at Isabella and Lila, who both grimaced back at her. Nick, she noticed, was watching and listening politely.

Jessica watched as Alison cleared her throat loudly and set down her glass. She nodded to Celine, who stood up. Curiosity rippled through the room. "Since most of us have been studying for exams, I held off telling anyone—I didn't want to disturb anyone's concentration, after all. But now it's time to let you all know that"—she turned and gestured dramatically toward Celine—"Celine's grandmother, Ms. Anabelle Boudreaux, has kindly offered to donate the funds needed to redecorate the Theta house parlor room!"

The room thundered with applause. Stunned, Jessica dropped her spoon into her half-eaten mocha mousse and watched in disbelief as most of her Theta sisters cheered and clapped. Celine stood with a shy, downcast expression and a demure smile, but Jessica saw right through her phony little act. She couldn't believe that others were buying into it. *Celine is about as sweet as a cobra—she wants something from the Thetas, I just know it.* Maybe she wanted to take over the whole house and fill the place with her psycho friends.

Alison held up her hand for silence. "Naturally we are all grateful. I think it is only fitting and proper that we invite Celine to join the Thetas." She beamed at Celine, who acted as if she were overcome with delight. Clasping a hand to her open mouth and widening her eyes, Celine ran forward to hug Alison.

Jessica wanted to gag. She shoved the dish of mousse away from her. This had to be a dream—a nightmare. No other explanation could make sense. How else could the Thetas even think of inviting deranged, trashy Celine Boudreaux to join their house? Celine, who had helped criminally insane William White torment and abduct Elizabeth. Not to mention all her own rotten tricks she had played on Elizabeth.

The rest of the Thetas don't know Celine like I do, Jessica thought savagely. *But they're going to find out all about her. I'll make sure of it.*

Everyone was whispering and talking at once, and the sound level was deafening. Some people were even arguing heatedly. Isabella and Lila had their heads together and were nodding vigorously. Jessica was ready to spring to her feet, demanding there be a vote, when Magda Halpern, president of the Thetas, saved her the trouble.

"We have to put this to a vote, Alison," Magda asserted quietly. "I'm sure you understand, Celine." She nodded politely in Celine's direction.

"I wouldn't want to join if everyone was against me," Celine simpered.

Some of the Thetas smiled appreciatively; a few frowned. Jessica glared around the room at the Celine supporters. *Traitors.*

"This is unbelievable!" Jessica seethed to Nick, her blue-green eyes stormy.

"If there are any suggestions on how to handle this proposition—" Magda began.

Jessica leapt to her feet. "I suggest we postpone this vote until we've discussed all the facts. After all, the Thetas have a tradition to uphold, Magda."

There was a smattering of applause. Celine's

smile dropped a notch, but she held her innocent-maiden pose.

Alison looked indignant. "Now, just a minute; I—"

Magda broke in neatly. "I have to agree with Jessica on this, Alison. Every Theta has a right to speak her mind. Now is not a good time for this—we should bring it up at our next house meeting." She sat down with an air of finality. Alison and Celine sat too and immediately put their heads together. Celine dabbed at her eyes with a napkin and made a tragic face. Jessica watched with disgust. Celine was a terrible actress.

Bruce Patman, who had been sitting quietly at Lila's side, suddenly spoke up. "Nothing like this ever happens at Sigma house—I mean, we never get so excited about stuff. You women are so emotional."

Jessica sent him a withering look.

Lila frowned at him. "Bruce, please. You're making things worse."

"The only thing that can make this night worse is if Celine really does join the Thetas," Isabella interjected with a toss of her shining dark hair.

"I'll second that." Lila shook her head and pushed her mousse away.

"I can't believe this, Jess." Isabella leaned forward, her gray eyes steely. "We can't let that little demon in, especially not after all the horrible things she did to Elizabeth. What's Alison thinking of? Surely she knows Celine almost got your sister killed."

Jessica shrugged and bit her lip.

"I can't believe Alison either," Lila commented. She flipped her hair over her shoulders. "I thought she had more class than to dump Celine on us."

Isabella leaned her chin on her hands. "This entire night has been a bust. That rich French food Alison served is sitting in my stomach like cement."

Jessica wadded up her napkin and slammed it onto the table. "I know what you mean. I think I'm going to be sick," she said in a low, dangerous voice. "Really I am. Either that or I'm going to strangle both Celine and Alison."

Nick, who had been sitting silently ever since Alison's announcement, spoke up. "Don't let it get to you, Jess. I'm sure everything will work out."

Jessica straightened and lifted her chin. "I doubt it. But thanks anyway. You were so quiet, I thought you might have fallen asleep."

"I tried not to," came his dry reply.

Isabella reached across to squeeze Jessica's hand. "Hang in there, Jess. Maybe Celine will get bored after a few of our meetings and quit on her own. Besides, she's not a member *yet*. Don't forget that."

Jessica took a sip of water. "I haven't forgotten, Izzy," she said calmly. "I know exactly how to keep Celine out of the Thetas." She tightened her jaw and squared her shoulders.

Isabella and Lila both turned to stare at her.

142

Jessica rose majestically to her feet. Every eye in the room seemed to swivel toward her. She inhaled deeply. "Magda," she called out in a clear, ringing voice. "I have something to say to everyone."

The babble in the room suddenly stopped. Magda peered at Jessica with quizzical eyes.

Jessica stared right at Celine. "Actually it's a question I have. Do we Thetas really want to let a cold-blooded murderer become one of our sisters?"

"Jessica is a liar!" Alison shouted over the sudden hubbub before Celine could open her mouth. "We all know Jessica herself can't be trusted. Her record isn't squeaky clean." Alison was on her feet, her eyes burning with outrage.

Celine tried to look helpless and pathetic. Let Alison defend her—it only made Celine seem more innocent.

Denise Waters spoke up. "Celine was involved with William White, who tried to kill Elizabeth, myself, and many of our friends. We can't ignore that, Alison."

"Celine has made amends," Alison cried. "She's a changed person now that she's free from William White. He manipulated poor Celine. And we can't forget that she tried to *save* Jessica's sister." She turned and pointed dramatically to Celine. "Do you know that William White almost succeeded in killing Celine too?"

Celine buried her face in her napkin and made

sobbing sounds. Alison patted her back and glared across the room at Jessica.

Jessica refused to back down. "You have no right attacking me, Alison. I'm only looking out for the Thetas. Elizabeth almost died because of Celine. And it's my duty as a member of the Thetas to warn my fellow sisters how dangerous Celine can be."

Alison started to speak again, but Magda jumped in. She stood and cleared her throat loudly in an effort to get everyone's attention. "I must remind you all that we will discuss Celine's nomination at our next meeting. This is not the time or place. But I do understand your concerns, Jessica." She sat down and motioned for Alison to sit as well.

Jessica nodded, but she didn't look happy. Watching Jessica huddle with her friends, Celine made a vow to herself. *You'll pay for that little speech, Miss Jessica. You'll be sorry you ever tangled with me.*

The noise in the room didn't subside. Everyone was talking at once. Celine barely listened to Alison's diatribe against Jessica, but instead she strained to hear bits of conversation that floated her way from the other Thetas.

"Did she really kill someone?"

"No, silly. She stopped that crazy guy from hurting Jessica's sister."

"Something's fishy about her story—"

"It's just gossip. Celine's just a victim herself."

Celine smiled. The damage wasn't as bad as she thought. Her mind was whirling as she plotted her next move. Celine had done a good job of looking crushed and pitiful. And Alison *was* a persuasive speaker. Certain Thetas were already sending sympathetic looks Celine's way. *My plan is going to work. Even Little Miss Snip can't stop me.*

Celine made her way around the tables, smiling and chatting to all the Thetas who seemed remotely friendly. Celine knew she had to work hard if she wanted to become a Theta, despite the fact that there were girls who were already on her side. Celine was so determined to win, she even restrained herself from flirting with the Thetas' dates—despite the fact that her dress was a definite drool magnet for males.

As Celine hugged Kimberly Schyler she discreetly surveyed the candlelit room. It was quite a spread. Real linen tablecloths, fine china, crystal goblets, and silver flatware—all worth a mint. If they got rid of the sappy music in the background, Theta house would almost be the spitting image of her favorite restaurant, Chez Emile, back at home.

There was money to burn in SVU, which fit into her plan perfectly. All these people in their designer dresses and expensive suits were going to advance Celine's cause, whether they knew it or not.

"I'm so excited for you," Kimberly gushed. "I can't wait to see the renovations. You'll make a terrific Theta, Celine."

"Why, thank you, sugar," Celine said demurely, eyeing Kimberly's date. Not bad, but too young and green for Celine. She couldn't resist, though, leaning across the table and plucking out a white carnation from the floral centerpiece. She tucked it into the low neckline of her tight-as-a-glove black velvet dress. Kimberly's date must have gotten an eyeful because he was red as a beet. "I appreciate your support. I just know y'all will love the new parlor my granny's paying for."

Of course no one had to know that the money wasn't coming from her witchy old granny. As Granny herself used to say, "Don't tell people what they don't need to know."

Celine waved to Alison, who threw Celine a big, encouraging smile. *Alison, poor thing, doesn't know anything about style,* Celine thought. *She looks like an old stick in that horrid brown dress of hers.* But that didn't matter—Alison would be useful for other things. Mandy Carmichael called to Celine. Celine hurried over, studiously avoiding the snots who were staring at her as if she were dirt. They were all Jessica Wakefield clones anyway.

After a few minutes of gab with Mandy, Celine moved on. *Chalk up one more for my side,* she crowed to herself gleefully.

There was one person she wouldn't avoid, and that was Jessica herself. Celine slithered toward Jessica's table. *Now's my chance to make her pay, Little Miss Thinks-she's-so-hot. That gorgeous Nick is perfect for my plan, and I'm going to snatch him right out from under her nose!*

"Why, Jessica," she dripped, tossing back her

146

mane of golden curls. "What a sweet-looking dress. And Nick Fox, my handsome assailant, don't you look good." Celine pulled up an empty chair close to Nick and turned to face him. She carefully ignored the daggers Isabella and Lila were shooting at her but kept an eye on them and Jessica.

"That dress is new, isn't it, Izzy?" Jessica said loudly, pointedly ignoring Celine.

Isabella answered smoothly, "This old thing?" She ran her hands down the rich, crimson brocade of her dress. "It's not as cute as your sheath."

Bruce Patman grinned and opened his mouth to speak until Lila elbowed him sharply. "I love those earrings, Isabella. They look stunning with your dark hair," Lila said pleasantly.

Isabella tossed her hair back to show off the dangly hoops of gold.

Celine pulled her chair even closer to Nick. "I'm so glad you came to our dinner." Celine smiled at him through her thick lashes. She lowered her voice seductively. "I must say, I was pleasantly surprised to see you." She stroked his arm with a slender hand, red nails gleaming.

"I'd say you're the person who's full of surprises, Celine. That was very generous of your grandmother to donate money to the Thetas." Nick seemed amused as he turned to face her. He was no fool, no pushover. Celine liked that.

"Why, thank you. If only other people would be generous to me, I would be so thrilled to become a

Theta—" Celine glanced at Jessica's rigid profile.

Nick didn't seem to hear Celine's last sentence. "Why are you surprised to see me here? You heard Alison invite me. It's not like I crashed the place."

"I wasn't thinking anything like that." She moistened her lips. "It's only that you seem like a man who'd rather spend his time at a real party."

"A real party?" Nick raised an eyebrow.

"You know," she breathed. "Parties where they don't just fill you with a little food and wine and think that's all there is to having a good time—parties where you can have some genuine *grown-up* fun."

"I know exactly what you mean," Nick said. His deep green eyes were sharp with interest. "I've yet to find that kind of party here at SVU."

"You haven't been hanging out with the right people, then," Celine flirted, shooting an evil look Jessica's way. "I'd be *happy* to take you partying, Nick. You just say the word." She leaned a little closer, showing her cleavage.

"The word is 'get lost,' Celine," Jessica interjected sharply. "Nobody wants to go to any party of yours." She glared at Celine.

Celine made her lower lip quiver pathetically for Nick's benefit. "You are so cruel, Jessica, and ignorant. You don't even know my friends. They happen to be very fine people." She pretended not to hear Isabella's loud snort.

Jessica smiled contemptuously. "We all know what your friends are like. Remember, many of us

148

had the *pleasure* of meeting William White." She glanced at Nick, her eyes shooting sparks. "Don't go anywhere with Celine, Nick. Bad things have a habit of happening around her."

Celine gritted her teeth but continued on in her most syrupy voice. "Can't Nick speak for himself, Jessica? Or are you afraid to let him?" With satisfaction she watched Jessica's face blanch and her eyes darken.

Nick seemed calm. His piercing eyes went from Jessica to Celine. When he spoke, his husky voice made Celine shiver. "Let's just cool it for now. We don't need any more bloodshed in this room. . . ." A faint smile appeared on his face. Celine's pulse began to pound. Nick really was just too adorable.

Celine rose grandly to her feet. "Never mind, I can be the bigger person. I'll leave. As my granny Boudreaux always says, a lady doesn't stay where she's not wanted." She smiled at Nick. "We'll meet again." She bent and whispered directly into Nick's ear, knowing he could smell her perfume. "I promise."

"Are you OK, Alex?" Noah asked, his eyes serious. "You've been acting like a zombie ever since Alison made that announcement about Celine. You shouldn't let Celine upset you so much. It's time to move on with your life."

Alex looked up in disbelief. "How can you say that, Noah? You were in the van when we all almost died. . . ." Alex felt her voice break. She shivered, though it wasn't cold outside. Wrapping her arms around herself, Alex lowered her head and trudged on.

"That was because of William White, though," he said reasonably. "I know Celine's no angel, but why not give her a break? Maybe she's changed." They headed toward the quad, leaving Theta house behind. Jessica wasn't the only one disgusted about Celine's nomination. Several other people, including Alex and Noah, had left the party early.

"You just don't understand, Noah," Alex said shakily. She stopped and brushed back the curtains of curly auburn hair falling around her face. "I worked so hard to get into the Thetas. And here comes Celine, with her shady past and all, who just buys her way in. It's not fair, Noah. Life just isn't fair." She closed her eyes and felt him pat her shoulder. The gesture was soothing and reminded her how kind and supportive Noah had always been. Maybe it was time to be honest with him.

"Noah," she said quickly before she could change her mind. "I've been having a rough time lately, and I know you've noticed how tense I've been. Recently everything's a struggle—my classes, the Thetas—and I'm totally overwhelmed. And I've been craving a drink. Actually I'd almost die for just one sip. Something to calm my nerves." Alex trembled as she tried to read Noah's face in the dark. The burden on her heart was lifted, and she felt instantly better just talking about her feelings.

There was a silence. Noah was slow to respond. "I'm shocked, Alex. I'm sorry to be blunt, but I can't understand why you'd want to drink again. Frustration with your classes and anger at Celine shouldn't be enough to push you over the edge. You've worked hard to get sober; just remember that. Drinking will only make you feel worse." Noah's tone was sharp and loud.

Alex couldn't help feeling a sense of betrayal. She had trusted Noah with her fears, and now he was turning her heart into ice. "I know that. That's why I told you about it. I thought you could help me fight my weakness. I thought you'd understand."

Noah frowned at her and took a step toward her. "I do understand, but I don't think you need sympathy right now. You need to face the facts—"

Alex struggled to catch her breath as she quickly pulled away. She was so furious, she didn't see where she was going and banged right into a lamppost. She could feel Noah staring at her as she rubbed her sore shoulder. The sudden physical pain kept her from crying. "No, Noah, I already know the facts," she said sarcastically. "Right now I just need your support."

"You're not looking for support; you want my pity," Noah snapped. "And I'm not about to give it to you. You're feeling sorry enough for yourself!"

"You obviously don't care about me!" Alex shouted.

Noah grew calmer. "I do care, but I have to wonder—"

"You wonder if I'll fall off the wagon," Alex cut him off, struggling not to break down. "Just because I confided in you . . . because I told you that I have an urge to drink. I didn't say I was going to *give in* to that urge. If you don't trust me, Noah, then I don't think we have anything to say to each other." Alex turned away from him and began running across the grass. She ignored Noah's shouts behind her and raced blindly past the dimly lit buildings.

I hate him, she told herself. He was so self-righteous and pompous. He didn't understand her feelings. Noah wasn't the person she thought he was. Alex's cheeks were wet, and she could scarcely breathe as she reached her dorm. Tears blurred her eyes as she stumbled toward her room. And waves of emotional pain made her dizzy.

Everything is wrong in my life, and Noah and I are through. Nothing will ever be right again.

This was one of the worst nights of Jessica's life. Theta house was her sanctuary, and now it would be ruined. How could the Thetas even think of inviting Celine to join them? *Celine is like a toxic spill—she'll ruin everything.*

"I can't believe I invited those traitorous Thetas—" she muttered under her breath. Right before Alison's announcement Jessica had happily asked her Theta sisters to attend Tom's surprise birthday party. Jessica had only been trying to liven up Elizabeth's little gathering. Her twin sister needed all the help she could get when it came to having fun. Now Jessica wished she could *un*invite the Thetas, with the exception, naturally, of her loyal friends.

Nick glanced at her from the corner of his eye but didn't say anything.

Jessica's stomach roiled in anger. *I bet Alison nominated Celine just to annoy me.* Alison had been so nasty when Jessica told everyone the truth about Celine. But the grossest part of the evening was when Celine threw herself at Nick, who didn't exactly push her away.

Jessica was glad she and Nick had left the dinner party early. She was too upset to deal with another minute of Alison and Celine. Jessica watched Nick's profile as he drove toward her dorm and decided that he had to know the facts about Celine. "Look, Nick," she began earnestly. "You may have thought I was exaggerating about Celine. . . ." Jessica gave him the details as briefly as possible. She didn't want to waste more time on Celine than she had to.

"That's a terrible story, Jess. But listen, maybe Celine's just a messed-up person who let a dominant, disturbed personality influence her in a bad way."

"You can't honestly feel *sorry* for Celine!" Jessica stared at him, her eyes glittering with outrage.

Nick held up a hand in front of his face in mock defense. "Don't attack me. Let me explain. Celine reminds me of an old friend of mine in L.A."

"A *friend?*" Jessica arched a suspicious brow. If this was going to be some tragic old-girlfriend story, she would jump right out of the car, even if it was going over fifty miles per hour. The last thing she needed to hear was that Celine reminded Nick of one of his lost loves.

"She *was* just a friend, but a close one," Nick insisted, shooting her a quick glance. "My friend was a mixed-up girl with a bad attitude. She also made plenty of enemies. Underneath, though, she was a good person. The nastiness was just an act."

"What was your friend's name?" Jessica asked, narrowing her eyes.

"That doesn't matter. What does matter is that people can change."

"So what happened to your *friend?*" Jessica interjected sarcastically, smoothing stray wisps back into her chignon. "Did she eventually become a saint or did she dedicate her life to helping troubled kids?"

Nick grinned, and she could see the white flash of his teeth in the dark. "Such cynicism, and at such a tender age. Actually my friend did turn her life around, but with the help of people who cared and saw through her attitude."

"People like you, right?" Jessica was scornful.

"Yeah," he agreed. "I helped her out. And I

think I could help Celine too." He looked serious.

Jessica bit her lip and fought back sudden tears. She was hugely disappointed. How could he choose Celine over her?

"Let's get one thing straight, Nick," Jessica began in a clipped, grim tone. She took a deep breath. "You can't be friends with both me *and* Celine, understand?"

Nick scowled. His emerald eyes darkened. "What are you saying?"

"You're either with me or with *her.* You can't have us both!"

Nick pulled into the parking lot of Dickenson Hall and stopped the car. "Jessica, if you don't trust me, this will never work. I don't like ultimatums." He stared straight ahead, his sensitive lips in a tight line.

Jessica threw him a pain-stricken look and leapt out of the car, slamming the door behind her.

Nick rolled down his window. "Jessica!"

Without saying a word, Jessica spun on her heel and ran blindly toward the dorm.

"Jessica—stop!" he called behind her.

Jessica kept going until she reached the door. Yanking it open, she raced inside and headed for her room.

I'll never see him again, she reassured her aching heart. Her eyes felt hot, but she knew she wouldn't break down. Anger was a good tear stopper. Nick was a player, a womanizer, and she deserved someone better than that. Jessica had had enough heartbreak in her past; she didn't need to add another name to the long list of men who had hurt her. A lineup of those men appeared before her mind's eye: Mike, James, Randy, Louis . . . and now Nick Fox? *No way—I'm not going to let another man trash my life and leave me to pick up the pieces.*

Chapter Eight

"Damn!" Nick pounded his fist on the dashboard as he nearly rear-ended a pickup that had suddenly stopped dead ahead. Swerving around the truck, he restrained himself from leaning on the horn. "Don't take your bad mood out on some stranger, Fox," he told himself.

He turned the radio to a heavy-metal station. The screech of the electric guitars reflected his feelings perfectly. He wanted to yell right along with the lead singer.

Sometimes this job really stinks! he thought, turning up the volume. He hated all the lies, all the pretending. He had to watch his step every single minute. He could never let down his guard. For example, he saw right through Celine and knew exactly what kind of person she was, but he couldn't share that insight with Jessica. Unfortunately Celine was perfect for his needs. She had practically handed

157

over the desired information gift wrapped. All he had to do was get a little closer to her. No problem there. Celine was more than eager.

Nick sighed and scratched his jaw. He told himself that playing Celine was just business. . . .

His eyes flicked to the rearview mirror, and he frowned. Two cars back he recognized the same rusted brown Ford that had been behind him for at least ten minutes now. When he glanced again, the Ford abruptly dimmed its lights.

Nick's adrenaline surged, and he suddenly shot forward and passed two cars. Without signaling he exited left onto the ramp and watched his mirror tensely. Sure enough, the brown Ford came barreling up, but then at the last minute it went right past the exit ramp and zoomed on ahead until it disappeared into the horizon. Relief turned Nick's muscles into wet tissue, and he wiped his brow on his sleeve.

He was lucky this time. The brown car had just been a fluke, one of those freaky things that happened without explanation. Nick felt his heart collapse back into his chest. He didn't blame himself for getting nervous—the people he dealt with were pretty rough customers. Which brought his thoughts back to Celine. Celine was his ace right now, and he had to stay in touch with her.

But what about Jessica? She was another story altogether. Jessica was under his skin. Even if he couldn't keep coming up with excuses to hang around her, he knew he couldn't stop seeing her.

Pictures of her flirting with him in the student center, laughing up at him on the roller coaster, kissing him on the quad, and looking like a haughty queen tonight flashed relentlessly through his brain. He could almost smell her fragrant long hair and taste the satiny sweetness of her lips.

No, he couldn't give up Jessica. He'd have to call her tomorrow and smooth things over. He would just have to see Celine on the sly. Celine was predatory and clever; she would be discreet if he wanted her to be. Celine was part of the game—she'd play by his rules.

Nick knew Jessica would be furious if she found out about his plans with Celine. She'd probably never want to see him again, and he couldn't let that happen. He would have to walk the delicate line between the two women and use all his balancing skills.

"If I'm not careful, I'm heading for a major collision here. And I can't mess up this job," Nick said out loud. "Neither Jessica nor Celine seems like a forgiving woman—they could both make my life miserable." Jessica was worth all the risk, though.

Nick caught a glimpse of his worried face in the rearview mirror. "Yeah, you should be nervous, buddy. You're already talking to yourself."

He sighed and ran a rough hand through his hair. "I'll just have to find a way to pull this one off." He plucked a long golden hair from the sleeve of his jacket and for a second held on to it tightly. He brushed the golden hair against his lips before releasing it.

Nick was definitely in a bind. He needed Celine, but he wanted Jessica Wakefield.

"Ouch! Go away, you stupid bird," Tom shouted at the squawking in his ear. If felt as if a huge crow were bouncing up and down on his arm and cawing so loudly that Tom's head was ready to shatter. He tried to shoo it away with his hand, but his arm didn't seem to be working too well. Surprisingly his head seemed to be made of eggshells too, and it would take very little to make his skull crack in two. . . . Tom moaned and buried his face in the pillows. It was all a dream; maybe now the crow would go away.

"Tombo, wake up," the crow insisted, shaking Tom's shoulder.

Tom opened one bleary eye and was sorry he did. The motion made him dizzy as he felt the room spin around him. Danny was hovering over him, an encouraging grin on his face. *Someone that happy first thing in the morning should be put behind bars,* Tom thought crossly. How could Danny look so perky and energetic when he'd consumed the same number of drinks Tom had the night before? It was a mystery.

A mystery that I'm not up to solving, Tom told himself, closing his eyes again. Maybe Danny would

go away. Next door some idiot was playing an old rock tune at full blast. The walls trembled as the bass boomed.

"Go break his CD player, will you?" Tom mumbled, motioning vaguely at Danny.

Danny ignored him. "Come on, Tom, let's get up and hit the pavement. Exercise will do you good, man. Nothing sweats out a hangover better than a good run." Danny dangled Tom's running shoes in front of his nose.

"Go away before I shoot you," Tom threatened softly so as not to bruise his pounding head. The sight of his shoes swinging back and forth in Danny's hand made him ill.

Danny sighed in sympathy and pulled up a chair. "I can't leave you lying here like an old sack of potatoes. You look pitiful."

"I am pitiful, so please take pity and leave me to my misery," Tom pleaded, covering his face with his arm. The sun was so bright through the window, it made his eyes water.

Danny shook his head. "I was going to wish you a happy birthday, but under the circumstances . . ."

Tom groaned. It was his birthday—twenty-one and legal. *Big whoop!* He had no family to celebrate with. He was all alone. Elizabeth hadn't even bothered to call, so maybe he didn't have a girlfriend either.

"I'm totally bummed," Tom announced. "I feel like staying in bed for the rest of my life." Tom rarely spilled out his feelings, but his misery was pressing him to speak. "I don't have any family. My girlfriend has abandoned me. I've just turned twenty-one—I'm a grown-up now—and it doesn't mean a thing to me."

Danny looked uneasy. "Come on, that's the hang-over talking. You have lots of things going for you. Your career plans, your friends, and Elizabeth—"

"Elizabeth doesn't seem to care all that much recently," Tom said in a gloomy voice. "She's been avoiding me lately. She doesn't have time to spend with me."

"C'mon, that's not true. You and Elizabeth are tighter than ever," Danny insisted, tapping his fingers nervously on his knee.

He's fidgeting because he knows it's true, Tom thought. "Whatever is going on with her, I know I'm not up to facing it," Tom said out loud. "You go running without me. I'll be fine once this hangover wears off."

"I hate to leave you like this," Danny said worriedly.

"Go ahead—maybe I'll change my mind and catch up with you," Tom forced a smile. *Just go on your run. I want to be alone.*

"OK, but I'm sorry about your hangover." Danny stood, fully attired in his sweats, and put Tom's shoes down. "I feel pretty guilty." He was peering down at Tom like a nurse checking on a patient.

162

"Don't worry about me," Tom said weakly. "I promise I'll feel better after a hot shower and some coffee. Last night was great—exactly what I needed—and right now I'm paying the price. It's no big deal. Go on your run. I'll be with you in spirit if not in the flesh." He flashed Danny a shaky smile.

Danny sighed, not seeming completely convinced. "OK, if you insist. But I'll check on you later," he promised as he let himself out.

Tom waved him off and closed his eyes with relief as the door shut softly behind his friend. It had been too much work to convince Danny he wasn't completely depressed. He was more tired than ever now. Even listening to earsplitting rock tunes was better than arguing with Danny about the quality of Tom's life.

For a moment there was blessed silence.

Two seconds later the neighbor cranked up a noisy rap tune.

Tom groaned and pulled the covers over his head.

Watch out, SVU, I'm on a roll, Celine gloated to herself. Her plan was moving right along. First she'd become a Theta, then she'd steal Nick Fox from Jessica, twin sister to Miss Goody Two-shoes. Defeating Jessica would be almost as good as defeating Elizabeth. And Jessica's vicious little scene last night only made Celine more determined.

Celine ran her fingers through her tangled curls and yawned. It was Saturday and almost noon, early for her, but she had things to do. She dialed Nick's number, toes curling in anticipation.

As his husky, silken voice answered, Celine felt chills run up her spine. Nick was definitely too hot for silly Jessica.

"It's me, honey—it's Celine," she crooned into the phone. "I needed someone to talk to. I hope you don't mind me calling."

Nick sounded confused. "What's up, Celine? Is something wrong?"

"Only that I'm lonely. Everyone hates me, Nick." She let her voice tremble. "Nobody wants me at Theta house. I feel like the whole world is against me."

"You've got Alison on your side," he said. "And other people too."

"I know, but I need something more personal," she breathed, and waited. When he didn't take the bait, she went on. "I just want someone to hold me—a friendly shoulder to cry on. You seem so kind and sweet—would you come over?"

Nick cleared his throat. "I can't today, Celine. Don't take this the wrong way, but I've got a lot to do."

"Oooh," she said in a sad voice. "I understand," she quavered.

"It doesn't mean we can't get together some other time," Nick added quickly.

Celine smiled seductively into the phone. "You promise?"

"Sure." He hesitated. "We'll talk soon, Celine."

Celine hung up. Nick didn't know it yet, but he was going to help her with plan B. *You'd better live up to your word, Mr. Fox. Because like it not, you're going to be mine.*

"I feel like we're having a secret affair," Elizabeth whispered to Mr. Conroy late Saturday morning. They were sitting in the nearly filled coffeehouse, preparing to continue their search. She smiled gently at Mr. Conroy to show that she was teasing.

Mr. Conroy gave her a startled look, and then he flushed a little.

Elizabeth was surprised. Quickly she explained, "I've spent more time with you these past few days than I have with my boyfriend." Not that Tom had even noticed. He'd been so down about turning twenty-one. But all that would change later that night.

Mr. Conroy looked morose as he rolled the salt-shaker between his hands. "I feel guilty taking you away from your boyfriend. He must hate me."

"Oh no," Elizabeth ad-libbed swiftly. "He's very understanding."

Mr. Conroy set the shaker down and gazed at her for a long second. "He's very lucky too," he said softly. "Any man would be blessed to have you in his life, Elizabeth."

Elizabeth didn't say anything. She just looked down at her folded hands and shifted in her chair.

"Anyway, the fates seem to be conspiring against

me. I wonder if my son and I will ever meet," Mr. Conroy said sadly.

Instantly Elizabeth felt her heart ache with sympathy. All these roadblocks were discouraging. She worked up a robust smile for Mr. Conroy's benefit. "Let's order and eat. A hot meal will get our brains working." Elizabeth pulled the menus from the table napkin holder and handed one to him.

He nodded silently and began skimming the menu. Elizabeth noticed he already had his cup of black coffee.

Elizabeth ordered a vegetarian omelet, fresh fruit, and milk.

Mr. Conroy said to the waitress, "I'll have the same, but skip the milk, please." His voice was leaden, and he shrank back in his seat.

Elizabeth inwardly groaned. Between Mr. Conroy and Tom, she was spending a lot of time trying to be Little Miss Sunshine. It was wearing her out.

"I'm afraid I'm wasting your time, Elizabeth. We've been banging our heads against a brick wall," Mr. Conroy suddenly said in a glum voice.

"It certainly feels like that," Elizabeth agreed tentatively.

"Maybe I should give up. Maybe my son doesn't want to see me after all these years. Maybe I'll just be messing up his life." Mr. Conroy rubbed his eyes tiredly.

Mr. Conroy was wrong . . . Elizabeth was sure of

166

it. Father and son were meant to be together. "I know you're discouraged, but I think we're really close. You know the old saying, 'It's always darkest before the dawn.' My gut tells me that's where we are now." She leaned forward, noting the flare of hope in Mr. Conroy's eyes. "Right before I break a story, I usually feel I've reached a dead end, that I'll never finish the story. And that's often when I get my best lead." She smiled eagerly at him. "So we can't give up now."

Mr. Conroy looked into her eyes, as if longing to be convinced. Before he could speak, the waitress served them their omelets and plates of melon and strawberries. Elizabeth was suddenly starving. Her stomach growled as she dug into her food. Yesterday she'd been so busy at the library, she hadn't had time for a decent meal.

"You could be right, Elizabeth." Mr. Conroy paused, a forkful of egg poised midair. "Maybe by this time next week my son and I will be having breakfast together right here."

Elizabeth beamed at him over her glass of milk. She was starting to feel better herself. Watching Mr. Conroy eat his breakfast, she wondered if his son would be as nice and sweet as Mr. Conroy.

"Do you have any idea what your son is like?" Elizabeth set down her glass and dabbed at her mouth with her napkin.

Mr. Conroy smiled dreamily. "Nothing concrete. I can only hope he's not too much like his old man.

If he's anything like his mother, he's hardworking, responsible, and thoughtful. I pray that he's happy and well adjusted. Somehow I picture him being bright and successful too." He met Elizabeth's interested gaze and raised one shoulder. "Whatever he's like, I know I'll love him."

Elizabeth felt a tickle of sentimental tears behind her lashes. Mr. Conroy sounded so caring and tenderhearted, she was bursting to take action and make his dreams come true. There had to be a way to find his missing child.

Unfortunately Elizabeth's ideas had all dried up.

Elizabeth swallowed another bite of omelet. She was cutting her slice of melon when she felt someone staring at her. Elizabeth looked up. Mr. Conroy was watching her with a funny expression.

"Is something wrong?" She was concerned.

Still gazing at her, he spoke softly. "No." Mr. Conroy smiled at her and reached across the table to squeeze her hand. "I just have a feeling that things are finally looking up."

"I should join a convent," Jessica said to no one in particular. "Considering my luck with men, that's probably the best place for me." She laughed in disgust at herself as she strolled to the window.

She popped open a can of diet soda and sat on the edge of her desk. Jessica had a major paper and a test coming up, but she couldn't concentrate. Besides, anything was better than studying. Even moping was preferable. *Stop thinking about Nick Fox,* she told herself, snapping her fingers. *He and Celine no longer count. Poof! They're gone—out of your mind!*

If only such magic worked, Jessica thought glumly as she sipped her soda. Last night's events scattered through her mind like confetti, and she couldn't stop obsessing about Nick Fox and Celine. Elizabeth had been up early, and Jessica hadn't had a chance to tell her that Celine might be joining the Thetas. She could just imagine Elizabeth's face when she heard the news.

The sun poured in through the window, and Jessica turned her face toward its warmth. *At least I can work on my tan,* she thought dully, setting down her soda and getting off the desk. The Thetas might be saddled with Hurricane Celine and Nick Fox probably wasn't as wonderful as she'd thought, but there was no reason she couldn't look good.

Jessica picked up her brush. Idly brushing her long, silken hair, she wondered if she should call Isabella or Lila. Both of them were as bummed as she was about Celine, but they might also have some choice criticisms of Nick. If she read them correctly, they had been charmed. But she knew they were still suspicious. And she wasn't in the mood to hear about it.

The phone jangled, making Jessica jump and drop her brush. *It's probably Isabella ready to lecture me on how Nick is bad news and how I should drop him like a hot brick.*

Scooping up the receiver, her heart began to

clamor. She immediately recognized the husky voice on the other end.

"Jess? It's Nick—did I wake you?" He sounded sweet and concerned.

Jessica tossed back her hair. "Don't be silly," she said in her coolest voice. "I've been up for hours." Or at least minutes, she amended to herself.

"I called to apologize about last night. You were right about Celine. I realize now she's into playing head games."

Jessica couldn't be won over that easily. "What changed your mind? Last night you were convinced she was a duplicate of your old friend."

Nick cleared his throat. "This morning she called with some fake story about needing a shoulder to cry on. She claimed she was feeling insecure about being accepted into the Thetas. She was pretty transparent, and I don't like manipulators."

Jessica felt an involuntary smile curl her lips. "What did you tell her?"

"I reminded her that Alison was her buddy and suggested she call her."

Jessica snickered. "She probably didn't like that."

Nick answered quickly. "Probably not, but that's her problem. I hope you can forgive me for buying into her act."

Jessica licked her lips and smiled to herself. "Maybe I can."

"Would a walk on the beach make it up to you? It's a beautiful day." Nick's voice dropped and became intimate. "I wouldn't mind spending time alone with you."

"All right. I was going to invite you to the surprise party my sister's throwing for her boyfriend. I hope you'll want to see me twice in one day—the party's tonight," Jessica said flirtatiously.

"Tell me about it when I pick you up. I'll be there in an hour."

Jessica's brain was whirling. "Make it two. I should warn you, though, the Thetas are coming tonight, and you know what that means—" She made a face, forgetting that Nick couldn't see her. "Celine will probably show up. She's like crabgrass, always around when you don't want her."

After hanging up the phone, Jessica danced around the room and opened her closet. She had to find the perfect beach-date outfit. She was glad that Nick had seen the light about witchy old Celine, but . . . suddenly she frowned, dangling a peach midriff top from her fingertip. Nick was just too changeable, too elusive. While he might be the most fascinating man she'd met in a long time, Jessica didn't like being kept in the dark.

Nick still hadn't told her about his past or anything specific about his personal life. His questions last night about drugs were unsettling too. And she couldn't forget about his beeper and . . . the gun. Nick's explanations were phony; Jessica was sure of it.

As a matter of fact, nothing about Nick Fox added

up. Nick acted edgy and was always looking over his shoulder. She knew he was hiding something. Now she just had to figure out what.

She frowned and bit her lip. She didn't want *her* men keeping secrets from her. The rest of the world could be shut out, but not Jessica Wakefield.

It was time for Nick to open up and spill his guts.

Chapter Nine

Stop torturing yourself, Elizabeth scolded herself. *You have a million things to do and no time to worry about poor Mr. Conroy.* Adjusting her baseball cap, Elizabeth scanned her list and started making check marks. The day was flying by too fast, and she felt her heart beat harder in her chest. What if she didn't get everything done in time?

Elizabeth shifted to a more comfortable position and leaned back against a tree. She was sitting in the middle of the quad because strategically it gave her an advantage. She had a lot of running around to do, and the quad was right in the middle of campus. A breeze tickled her nose with the faint scent of fresh-mown grass. Hazy pictures of a picnic in the park with a glorious sundown in the background danced before her. She sighed a heartfelt sigh. *Maybe I should have planned a private birthday celebration with just me and Tom,* she thought dreamily, looking off into space.

"Hey, Elizabeth." Winston Egbert interrupted her fantasies of Tom. "I didn't startle you, did I? You looked lost in thought." He was carrying a folder and wore a pencil tucked behind his ear.

Elizabeth rose to her feet and stretched. "Actually I was lost in worry, Winston. I keep thinking I've forgotten something important."

Winston nodded sagely. "I know the feeling. I wake up like that almost every day." He suddenly grinned at her. "By the way, I can't wait until tonight. I promise I won't let you down, Liz. I'll be best DJ you've ever seen."

"I have complete faith in you," she assured him with a sincere smile. Winston was perfect for the role of DJ. Elizabeth and Jessica had known Winston since they were little kids, and he'd always been the class clown . . . a natural comic. "But I'm worried how the rest of Tom's party is going to turn out." She frowned down at her list.

"Relax—everything will work out," Winston said cheerfully. "Besides," he added, thumping his chest, "I've got everything under control." He handed her a piece of paper from his folder. "I've got twenty-one yeses, four maybes, and only three nos. I wrote it all down for you."

"That's great, Win! Now I sort of have an idea of our guest list." Elizabeth skimmed the list and inserted it into her notebook. "Unfortunately, in a moment of weakness I told Jessica she could invite a few of her friends."

174

Winston raised his eyebrows. "Uh-oh."

"Exactly." Elizabeth looked dazed. "Oh, well, I can't worry about that now. Are you sure you don't mind playing DJ tonight?" Her eyes were earnest. "It won't interfere with you having fun, will it?"

"Are you kidding?" Winston crowed. "That is my idea of having fun. I'm a natural at this kind of thing." He did a little John Travolta swivel, jabbing his hand down and up wildly. "Just call me Mr. *Saturday Night Fever* Man!" His pencil sprang from behind his ear and bounced to the pavement. Winston, pretending to break-dance, hit the ground in a floppy push-up and picked up the pencil with his teeth. He jumped to his feet and swirled the pencil around in a choppy version of the Hustle.

Elizabeth threw back her head and laughed. The icy lump in her stomach was starting to melt. Winston would be wonderful at loosening up a crowd. He had already made her feel better. "You're better than a natural, Win—you're a pro! I can't wait to see you in action tonight."

Winston made a mock bow, a giant smile splitting his face. "I'll do you proud, Elizabeth. I promise. I'll bring a bunch of my CDs and I've asked Denise to contribute a few of hers—even if she is totally fixated on classic rock."

"Great," Elizabeth said, scratching down a few more notes. "I'll bring our player and some music too. I'd better move it—I have a million errands to run, and I still have to help Nina with the decorations.

175

See you tonight, Winston. And thanks for everything."

Winston was several yards away when he yelled, "Hey, if you need any more help, just call me!" He did another crazy disco spin and waved crazily.

Elizabeth turned, smiled broadly, and waved enthusiastically back at him. A surge of optimism made her walk more jauntily. *Maybe the party won't be a dismal failure after all,* she thought with sudden hopefulness. Elizabeth glanced at her watch; she should call Tom soon. The nearest phone was in the snack bar, and if she hurried, she would be talking to Tom in less than ten minutes. She missed him with a sharp intensity that almost took her breath away.

Elizabeth dialed quickly. "Be home, Tom," she whispered to herself. She only wanted to hear his voice.

The second she heard Tom answer, "Elizabeth who?" Elizabeth felt her heart plunge. He was still in a strange mood, and now he was irritated with *her*.

"I'm sorry, Tom. I didn't mean to neglect you—" she said in her most appeasing voice.

"Thanks, Liz, but you didn't have to make this little duty call," he cut her off abruptly. Elizabeth stared at the receiver in shock. Snappish behavior was so unlike Tom. She had obviously underestimated how bad Tom's mood really was. He rarely got upset over minor issues, and he'd never before been angry at her for having too full a schedule. Tom had always been very understanding.

"This isn't a duty call. I really, really missed you.

I didn't mean to get so caught up in . . . stuff," Elizabeth pleaded, knowing her explanation sounded lame.

"Look," Tom said in a heavy voice. "You don't have to baby me. If you have better things to do, I'd rather you do them."

Elizabeth had to pinch herself. Was this really the Tom Watts she knew—this cranky stranger who sounded like Oscar the Grouch? "There's nothing I'd rather be doing. I wanted to hear your voice. Honest." She allowed a small sigh to escape her lips. "I was going to sing 'Happy Birthday,' but you're already disgusted with me," she cracked, trying to lighten the moment.

Tom sighed. "I thought you were avoiding me, Elizabeth."

"I wish you knew how sorry I am. You have every right to be angry with me. . . ." Elizabeth felt her voice quiver. It was more extreme than she'd thought. She had hurt Tom's feelings and made him feel abandoned!

"I'm not mad at you. I've been in a rotten mood about my birthday, and not seeing you just made it a little worse. That's all."

"I should have been more sensitive." Elizabeth felt terrible. Tom had really needed her and she had failed him. Maybe this party idea wasn't so great after all. She plunged ahead. "I hope you're up to a romantic birthday dinner tonight, just the two of us. I thought we could celebrate over a candlelit gourmet meal—my treat." She held her breath, hoping he would say yes.

Tom hesitated. "You shouldn't go to a lot of trouble. I probably won't be the best company tonight."

"A great meal will make you feel better. I just know it," Elizabeth coaxed. She crossed her fingers. "I'd love to pamper you tonight. After all, it's your birthday. Please say you'll go."

"I don't deserve to be spoiled. . . ." Tom sounded as if he were weakening.

"I think we both deserve a special night out. C'mon, Tom." Elizabeth was firm. She wasn't going to take no for an answer. "We'll have a great time, you'll see. Can I pick you up at a quarter to eight?"

Tom finally caved in, and as she hung up the phone Elizabeth stared bleakly down at the ground. What if this surprise party thing backfired? She massaged her forehead wearily. *Don't think like that. Be positive. Tom's mood is catching, that's all. This party will be a success.*

Alex couldn't breathe. Her nose was swollen and her throat was raw. Dabbing at her aching eyes with a limp, tattered tissue, she tried to take a breath. Instead another river of tears welled up and poured down her cheeks. The curtains were tightly drawn because she couldn't bear to see what a lovely, sunny day it was outside. She had the radio tuned to a mellow pop station, and they'd been playing tragic love songs for over an hour. Alex hadn't been out of bed all morning. She hadn't showered or brushed her teeth. It was lunchtime and she wasn't even hungry.

Turning to sob into her pillow, she wished she had a magic lantern with her own personal genie in it. She wouldn't even ask for three wishes. She needed only one wish—for her entire life to be fixed!

Everything is such a mess, Alex thought drearily as she turned to stare up at the ceiling. There was a crack in the plaster that formed an interesting design. It curved into the shape of a wizened little gnome. "That's probably what I look like now—an ugly old gnome," Alex whimpered softly. She hadn't worked up enough courage to glance in the mirror. Crying for hours did little to enhance a person's appearance.

She thought about her exams and her fight with Noah, and a new flood of tears trickled down her sticky, hot cheeks. He hadn't even bothered to call her today.

Alex's roommate, Trina, walked in at that very moment. She stared down in dismay at Alex's weeping, prone form. "What on earth is wrong with you, Alex?" Trina stepped closer, and Alex could smell her expensive perfume. Trina looked pretty and well dressed, and she was wearing perfectly applied makeup. Even her hair was glossy and curled. The sight of Trina made Alex feel worse than ever. Trina opened the curtains, allowing a stream of sunshine to pour in.

Alex groaned and closed her eyes.

Trina clicked off the radio. "Just what you *don't* need—tearjerker music."

Alex tried to speak, but only a hoarse cough came out.

Trina pulled up a chair and patted Alex's shoulder. "Let me guess—we're talking man troubles, aren't we?" She smoothed Alex's hair from her face.

Alex nodded mutely, her eyes red and burning. She and Trina had always been friendly, but never that close. While they were comfortable sharing the casual day-to-day stuff of their lives, they rarely divulged anything deeper. But now Alex was too depressed to hold back, and there was no one else to talk to.

"I wish I'd known you were so upset. When I left this morning, I just thought you were sleeping in." Trina sounded dismayed. But Alex had intentionally hidden her distress from her roommate and had buried her tear-puffed face into her pillow when Trina had gotten up.

"Don't move—I'll be right back." Trina got up and was back in less than a minute. She was carrying a cool, damp washcloth and a glass of water. She held the cloth to Alex's head and made her sit up and drink the water. "If you can wait a second, I'll go down to the cafeteria and bring you back a cup of coffee."

Alex shook her head. "Thanks, Treen, but this is fine." Her voice was husky and thick. After gulping down a few swallows of water, she nodded. She did feel a little better. "It's not just Noah, though we did have a major fight last night," Alex explained over a swollen throat. "It's *everything*. My life is completely messed up. I should just climb into a hole and never come out."

"It can't be that bad. You totally underestimate yourself, Alex." Trina spoke firmly and confidently. "You've got so much going for you. You're pretty, nice, and well liked. You do well academically, and you and Noah *will* patch things up. He's a super guy, and he adores you." Trina opened a desk drawer and handed Alex a fresh box of tissues.

Alex set down the glass of water and blew her nose. "Thanks for trying to make me feel better, but you don't know everything that's bothering me. First I'm flunking some of my classes, then Noah and I have this major blowout, and worse—Celine Boudreaux is back. And she's trying to join the Thetas." Alex felt another rush of despair. Too many things were going wrong in her life. If only she could run far away from SVU. If only she could escape being Alexandra Rollins.

For a second Trina looked dazed. "Wow, that is pretty bad." Then she frowned to herself and swiftly changed gears. "But life as we know it is not over, Alex. You can ignore Celine, ask your professors for help with the subjects you're struggling with, and make up with Noah." Trina spoke with authority as she looked at Alex with easy assurance. "I know everything will work out for you, Alex. I have complete confidence in you."

"I'm glad someone does," Alex said with a weak smile. She sat up and swung her legs out of bed. "Thanks for being a friend, Trina."

Trina eyed her closely before standing up. "If you promise not to crawl back into bed the second I'm out of here, I'll leave you alone. I'm going to the lounge to meet some people for a study session."

"Go ahead. I'll be fine." She gave Trina a watery grin. "I guess I should start getting ready for the surprise party I'm going to. Time to make myself look human."

"A party is just the thing you need to perk you up."

Alex sat staring blankly as the door shut behind Trina. She raked her fingers through her long, wavy auburn hair, working through the tangles. Massaging her throbbing temples, she felt some of her energy wilt. Maybe Trina was right—maybe the party would help her mood.

Pull yourself together and make yourself look gorgeous. You don't need Noah to have an excellent time.

She didn't need anyone to make her feel better. Alex knew how to have fun on her own.

The surf crashed against the sand, spewing foam against the rocks. Seagulls screeched and dive-bombed overhead, and the air was pleasantly salty. Jessica gathered up shells every few inches, only to put them back down a few feet later. The sun caressed her bare arms and she hugged herself, feeling wonderfully alive and happy. Nick trailed not far behind her, throwing bread crumbs from one of the sandwiches he had packed to the gulls. So far they'd had a perfect day. Jessica felt dreamy, all her doubts temporarily put aside.

Jessica wore a cropped peach shirt with matching shorts and carried her sandals in her hands. Suddenly she broke into a run and flew lightly over the sand, her feet easily skimming the ground. Her long hair bannered out behind her, and she laughed at Nick over her shoulder.

In seconds Nick was at her side, not even breathing hard. "Hey," he said, jogging beside her. "Wild child, are you going to keep running until one of us drops? Why don't you come back with me and have a cola?"

Jessica grinned and came to a stop. She knelt, scooped up a handful of wet, dripping seaweed, and draped it over his bare shoulders. She cocked her head to one side and nodded playfully. "Very chic—you could be on the cover of *New Man's Fashions*."

Nick chuckled and pulled off the soggy weeds. "Oh yeah, now you're asking for trouble." He raised the clump of seaweed over her head and pretended to trickle it onto her hair.

Jessica shrieked and ducked, but not before Nick had her thrown over his shoulder in a fireman's hold.

"Hey." She pounded on his back. "You better

not do what I think you're going to do or you're a dead man!"

Nick strode toward the water, apparently oblivious to Jessica's struggles. Laughing softly, he merely adjusted his hold.

"I mean it, Nick Fox! You throw me in and you are *d-e-a-d!*" Jessica shouted, laughing hysterically and squirming in his arms.

Nick only grinned wickedly and stepped through the water, stopping when it was knee deep. Easily he slid her down so that she was cradled in his arms. He held her over the glittering, cool Pacific.

She looked up at him, her face flushed and her blue-green eyes fierce. "Don't you dare. You wouldn't, would you?" she amended, casting him a playfully pitiful look.

For a long moment their eyes locked, and the world began to recede. He bent down to kiss her nose, breaking the intense moment. "No," he whispered. "I wouldn't." He carried her back to the sand and gently deposited her onto the ground.

Jessica took a deep breath and tried to tame her golden hair by smoothing it back behind her ears. She knew Nick was watching her, and she threw him a lighthearted smile. He was still very much an enigma, but she was getting closer to the real Nick. Her heart told her that he was beginning to really care about her, that he would eventually open up. Meanwhile Jessica couldn't take her eyes off him. He was gorgeous in his cutoffs, with the sun turning his skin honey brown and his eyes glass green.

He caught her hand in his, and they began walking slowly back to their blanket. Nick's hand was warm and strong, and Jessica liked the natural way he had reached for her hand. She examined his profile and tried to read him. Did he really like her as much as he seemed to or was she just fooling herself? After all, Jessica knew that her record for judging men wasn't great.

As if he felt her stare, Nick slid his glance toward hers. He smiled slowly and sensuously before pulling her close to him. His bare skin was smooth and warm against hers. And he moved in for a kiss that was as slow, warm, and sweet as the sea breeze brushing against their bodies.

Nick released Jessica with apparent reluctance and sighed to himself. He brushed away a strand of hair that had blown against her mouth and reached for her hand again. "So, wild child, I hope you're hungry. I brought the kind of food I thought you'd like."

"Really?" Jessica's face brightened with curiosity.

"Smoked turkey, goat cheese, and spicy mustard on French bread," he announced, watching her reaction.

Jessica beamed. "Somehow you know my tastes pretty well." She looked up at him through her lashes. "So far you've guessed that I like action and excitement, that I detest Celine, and that I love smoked turkey and goat-cheese sandwiches." She moistened her lips coquettishly. "Your record is perfect."

"I told you, Jess. We're kindred spirits." He squinted down at her, his heavy lashes squeezing out the sun.

They sauntered toward their blanket. Jessica lowered herself gracefully and stretched out her legs. "If we're kindred spirits, does that mean you'll go with me to my sister's party?"

Nick sat down next to her and opened the cooler. "Is that the surprise birthday party for your sister's boyfriend—what's his name, Tom? Sure, I'll go. It sounds like fun. As long as I'm not at the receiving end of surprise parties, I love them."

Jessica took the diet cola from him and drank thirstily before answering. She darted him an admiring look. "You have an amazing memory for names and facts. I could repeat something a hundred times to most of the guys I've dated and they'd never remember it. Unless it was the score of some ball game or the name of an engine part, most of them had selective memories."

Nick set down his soda and doodled in the sand with his finger. "I guess I'm different," he said casually.

Before she could think about what she was doing, Jessica reached over and kissed his cheek.

He looked up, seeming surprised.

Jessica shrugged. "I like that you're different," she explained simply. "I like everything about you—except for certain mysterious aspects. Why don't you ever talk about yourself?"

186

Nick twitched his shoulders. "I told you to be patient." He slid his arm around her shoulders. "Let's talk about something more interesting." He pulled her closer. "I'd rather hear all about Jessica Wakefield," he murmured, his lips brushing her cheek.

As if on cue, a shrill ring bleated into the air. The blanket vibrated, and Nick swiftly uncovered and pulled out his cellular phone.

He picked it up. "Yeah," he answered in a strange, clipped tone.

Nick's expression was suddenly masked, his green eyes cool and distant. "I'm sorry, Jess, but I have to take this call—in private."

When I'm queen . . . I mean, president . . . of the Thetas, I'm going to turn that little old sorority upside down. First she'd get rid of the lower-class element, like Jessica Wakefield, Isabella Ricci, and all the other bimbos who tried to keep her out. And she couldn't wait till Miss Priss Elizabeth found out she'd booted her precious sister from the sorority. Celine gave a small, pleasant shiver of delight, imagining Elizabeth's outrage. Things were definitely going to change at SVU once Celine was in charge of things.

Celine smiled into space, her eyes dazzled by the vision. She took a long puff on her cigarette, ignoring the ashes scattering to the floor. What did she care? She would be moving out of this crummy place soon anyway.

Everything was going Celine's way. Even Nick

Fox was falling into her hands like a juicy peach. He hadn't been able to take his eyes off her last night. He was adorable too, with that sexy voice and incredible body. She liked the reckless, rough quality he exuded. Celine put out her cigarette and licked her lips.

Nick was definitely in Celine's league, unlike most of the boys around SVU.

A knock on the door brought Celine to her feet. "It's Alison," called a familiar voice. "Are you home, Celine?"

"It's good to see you, sugar." Celine smiled broadly at Alison as she motioned her in. Good old Alison was Celine's ace in the hole.

"I'm happy to see that you haven't let Jessica ruin your mood. She was totally out of line last night. Why Magda doesn't expel her from the Thetas is beyond me." Alison sat primly on the chair while Celine stretched out across her unmade bed. Celine was careful not to disturb the curlers in her hair.

Celine's powder blue eyes lit with irritation. "Little Miss Jessica sure tried to mess up everything, didn't she?" She crossed her legs and adjusted a pillow behind her back. "Don't you worry, Alison. With my help you won't be burdened with her much longer."

Alison sat up straighter. Her thin lips spread into a smile. "That would be wonderful, Celine. Jessica has always been a weight around my neck. I'd love to get rid of her." She scooted the chair closer to Celine. "What did you have in mind?"

"Jessica is a low-class troublemaker. Once I'm a Theta, I'm sure I can convince the other girls they'd be better off without her."

"Don't forget, she does have a few friends in the house," Alison warned.

Celine smirked. "But not everyone likes her. The Thetas will toss her out, you'll see." Celine reached across the nightstand and lit another cigarette. "First, though, I'm going to teach her a little lesson. That gorgeous hunk of man she brought to the party last night is ripe for the taking." She winked at Alison, whose smile was getting bigger. "Nick Fox is going to be mine."

"Has he asked you out?" Alison breathed, leaning forward eagerly.

Celine smiled. "Not yet. I called Nick this morning, told him how bad I felt about last night—with all those mean girls picking on me." Celine blew a ring of smoke. "Men just love playing protector. I'd knew he'd feel sorry for me."

"What happened—did he fall for it?" Alison's eyes sparkled. Her pale face was flushed.

Celine hugged herself. "Of course he did," she purred. "He was as sweet as pie. He promised he'd come see me soon."

"I'm thrilled for you, Celine," Alison said. "And don't you worry about the Thetas. They'll vote you in."

Celine pulled her robe closer and sat up. She ground out the cigarette butt and opened her mini-refrigerator for two cans of soda. Celine handed one to Alison. "I have complete confidence in you, Alison. I can't wait to be a Theta."

"You can count on me," Alison promised as she daintily sipped her drink.

An unholy gleam came into Celine's eyes. "I just had a thought. I'll be seeing Nick at Princess Pill's little party tonight. Jessica *did* invite all the Thetas, didn't she?" Celine said confidently as she began taking out her curlers. *I'll make Nick mine tonight. Winner takes all,* she crowed to herself.

"Well, good luck, Celine. You must promise to give me all the juicy details tomorrow." And with that Alison stood up and walked out the door.

"That went well," Celine said out loud to herself. She smiled as she kicked the curlers from under her feet.

Celine would make a grand entrance at the party tonight. Just let them try and throw her out. Elizabeth wasn't the type to make a scene. She'd probably turn green. But she'd just pretend nothing was wrong.

Maybe Tom Watts would be glad to see her. Celine had once had a flirtation with Tom, and he couldn't be totally immune to her charms. Elizabeth couldn't have ruined him completely, after all.

What a scream if she stole both of the Wakefield twins' men! Celine laughed out loud. She could just see Jessica's face curdle with jealousy as Celine waltzed off with Nick. She could hardly wait.

A glance at her clock reminded her she had to get moving. If she planned to make Nick Fox fall totally in love with her and make a huge entrance at Elizabeth's party, she had to get started on her beauty regime.

Celine opened a bureau drawer and pulled out an enormous assortment of makeup and hair accessories. Her makeup bag weighed at least ten pounds. She had about five hours to get ready, just barely enough time. Natural beauty took a long time to achieve. As Granny Boudreaux always said, *Beauty may be only skin deep, but men aren't interested in what your bones look like.*

Chapter Ten

"Look out!" Elizabeth almost fell off the chair she was standing on. She waved her arms wildly, and the blue paper streamer and roll of tape she was holding dropped out of her hands. She looked across the room at Nina, who was also standing on a chair and holding the other end of the streamer. "Sorry, Nina." Elizabeth sighed. "At this rate we'll never get the room done in time for tonight. I'm all thumbs for some reason." She climbed down from the chair to retrieve the streamer and tape.

Nina flashed her a sympathetic smile. "It's understandable. You're throwing a huge party for the man you love. And to top it all off—it's a surprise party, which makes your planning even more complicated." She secured her end of the streamer with tape.

Elizabeth arched a wry eyebrow. "That's the problem—I'm trying to forget what a huge undertaking this is. If only I can keep telling myself that this is just a little celebration and no big deal, I can handle it. But every time I start imagining all the people showing up and Tom's reaction . . . I'm making myself crazy!"

"Is Tom still in a weird mood?" Nina looked across at her, concern in her wide brown eyes.

Elizabeth nodded and scooted her chair a few feet over. She had rented the Blue Room at La Casa Blanca. The room had deep blue carpeting and one glassed-in wall that overlooked the ocean. Neither she nor Nina had had much time to admire the spectacular view. Tables with cream-colored tablecloths and blue napkins were already set.

Elizabeth and Nina had planned to fan the streamers around the room. All the ends would meet in the center of the ceiling, where twenty-one silver and blue *Happy Birthday, Tom!* balloons would be clustered. Elizabeth leaned back and studied what they had accomplished so far. One-third of the room was brightly festooned in silver and blue streamers. She stopped to rub her stiff neck and sighed. They still had a lot of work ahead of them before the room would be ready.

Nina interrupted her thoughts. "Why's he so blue?" Nina shifted her chair and selected the roll of silver streamers. She tossed the other end to Elizabeth, who caught it easily.

Elizabeth shrugged. "I know he's sad that he doesn't have any family to celebrate his birthday with him. But I think it's more than that." She pulled off a strip of tape. "Tom told me he needs more support than he's been getting, especially from me." Elizabeth frowned.

"But you're one of the most giving and sensitive people I know," Nina insisted. Her beaded braids tinkled musically as she reached up with another streamer.

Elizabeth blew back her bangs wearily. "Not lately. I've been so involved with Mr. Conroy and this party that I've neglected him."

"What ever happened with Mr. Conroy and his son? Did you find him?" Nina looked curious.

"Nope," Elizabeth said in a depressed voice. "My judgment is off-kilter about everything these days. I was so sure I could help Mr. Conroy, but I completely failed. What if I'm wrong about this party too? What if it only irritates Tom, makes him more upset?"

Nina climbed down from her chair and walked over to the helium pump. "I think this party is just the thing he needs. Honestly, Liz, don't worry so much." She held up a bunch of the flat silver balloons. "Want to do these for a change of pace?"

Elizabeth nodded, tucking stray hairs back into her French braid. "Sounds good to me." She climbed down and picked up a few balloons. "I hope you're right about Tom. I still feel bad about Mr. Conroy, though."

The door suddenly swung open and Mr. Perryman, the restaurant manager, poked his head in. Behind

194

him a floridly painted face with a big red nose and an orange fright wig peeked in. Nina and Elizabeth exchanged surprised glances.

"Excuse me, ladies, but did you hire Nobbo the Clown for your party tonight?" Mr. Perryman, his eyes blinking rapidly, looked nervous. The clown came closer to the door and waved at them, grinning and fluttering his painted eyebrows.

Elizabeth couldn't hold back a giggle. The image of a clown waltzing into Tom's party made her giddy. She could just see Tom's grim face as the clown squirted him with water from a phony flower or tried to tickle him with a big feather duster.

"No, we didn't," Elizabeth said solemnly. "I can assure you we absolutely, positively did not hire Nobbo."

Mr. Perryman sighed, and Nobbo made a mock sad face. "Oh, thank goodness," Mr. Perryman said anxiously. "Nobbo must have the wrong restaurant." With that he closed the door.

Elizabeth and Nina instantly cracked up. They laughed so hard that they had to hold their stomachs. Every time their eyes met, they laughed even harder.

Elizabeth wiped her eyes. "I really needed that. Can you just imagine Nobbo and his big shoes trying to entertain Tom?"

Both girls surrendered to more giggles. Minutes later Elizabeth finally straightened and sobered up. "I guess we'd better get back to work or our guests will be hanging streamers with us."

"Actually, Liz," Nina began. "I have to go. I have an appointment at the Elan Hair Salon. When you see me next, I'll be a new woman." Nina tossed her braids and grinned. "No more braids."

Elizabeth gave her a quick hug. "Just promise you won't be late to the party, Nina. With or without your braids, I'm going to need as much support as I can get."

Jessica smiled excitedly at Nick as they mounted the steps to La Casa Blanca restaurant. She heard a bird that sounded like an owl hoot from somewhere in the dark. The moon was enormous and golden, and its light shimmered out onto the ocean. *Liz was right—this place is incredible.*

Jessica held Nick's arm as they glided through the doors. In khaki slacks and a sports jacket, Nick was sleek and elegant. His tan contrasted perfectly with the white shirt he was wearing. He was clean shaven but had that dark, shadowy look around his jaw that she loved. His thick, wavy hair was casual and sexy as it hung loose around his collar.

"If I didn't tell you before, Jess, you look beautiful," Nick said, gazing down into her eyes.

"You did mention it, but I don't mind hearing it again," Jessica retorted seductively, her sea-colored eyes shining softly. A black velvet headband kept her hair back, but long, golden wisps floated stubbornly over her shoulder. She impatiently brushed them back. Jessica had put a lot of thought into her outfit, not wanting to appear as if she were trying to up-stage Elizabeth but definitely wanting to look irre-sistible to Nick. She had selected her slinky backless black dress and had borrowed Lila's silk stole. Wearing black sandals with absurdly high heels had completed the ensemble.

"Tonight's the night, Jess. I can't wait to meet your twin. What's her boyfriend—the guest of honor—like?" Nick asked casually, his eyes checking out the restaurant.

Jessica shrugged. "Tom? He's OK. Not my type, of course. He's too serious and intense for me." She twinkled mischievously up at him. "He is very cute, though. We Wakefield women have very good taste in men."

Nick grinned at her. "Why, thanks—I'll take any compliment I can get."

As they entered the main dining area Nick whis-pered down to Jessica, his breath pleasantly tickling her ear, "I guess I better brace myself. I don't know if I can handle being around two Wakefield women. One alone is a handful."

Jessica smirked and adjusted her stole.

The maître d' gestured and led them to the back of the restaurant. They passed by candlelit tables and well-dressed diners. The air was heady with luscious aromas of seafood and spices wafting from the kitchen. A miniature waterfall surrounded by lush plants sparkled in the center of the restau-rant. The ceiling was painted like a night sky, complete with stars, clouds, and a half-moon.

"Nice place," Nick murmured, taking in the sights.

Jessica nodded. "Elizabeth chose well. I hope Tom appreciates it."

"I'm sure he will," Nick said. "What's not to like?"

Just then a feminine voice spoke behind them. "Jessica, what perfect timing." It was Lila Fowler, looking stunning and regal. "I'm glad we ran into each other," Lila said, walking up beside Nick and Jessica. She arched a brow and sent Jessica a significant glance, which Jessica chose to ignore. Lila seemed to be dying to get a second look at Nick. Probably because she didn't get a chance to grill him at Alison's party last night. One thing Jessica did not need was Lila acting like a mother hen.

Another voice called behind them. "Lila, Jessica— you two look great." Bruce Patman smiled suavely as he strolled up beside them. *Bruce is dashing and well groomed*, Jessica thought. *But he can't hold a candle to Nick, even if Bruce's clothes* do *come from the most expensive shops in town.* Bruce never bought off the rack; he and Lila were two of a kind in many ways.

Jessica watched Bruce's eyes quickly assess the cut and quality of Nick's clothes. Jessica rolled her eyes. Bruce was so shallow. It was hard to believe she'd once dated him briefly back in high school.

Nick was charming Bruce and Lila both and with great ease. Jessica loved it. The two haughtiest people in Sweet Valley were being bowled over by a man with a questionable past. Squelching a giggle, she followed the three of them into the Blue Room.

The room was packed and noisy. Jessica's eyes widened as she took in the spread of food and drinks; Elizabeth had really outdone herself. There had to be at least fifty people milling around and dancing. Winston was bopping and jiving around the CD player, handling the crowd with cheerful ease. Contemporary rock music throbbed from the speakers. Denise was dancing rhythmically beside him and handing him CDs. Petite and beautiful, she was perfectly relaxed in front of an audience.

The music was suddenly muted, and Winston waved his arms and called out for silence. "Danny tells me we have about fifteen minutes. I'll give everyone the countdown as we get closer to Tom's arrival."

Then the party resumed, but on a much quieter scale. Danny adjusted the banner that read *Surprise on Your 21st Birthday, Tom* and eyed his watch every two seconds. A small group from WSVU was waiting near the door with handfuls of confetti. Jessica watched as Bruce talked to a few other Sigmas.

"I can't believe what I'm seeing." Jessica did a double take.

"What?" Nick followed her gaze inquisitively.

"Todd Wilkins is here." Jessica looked amazed. "Only my sister would invite her ex-boyfriend to her present boyfriend's party." She stared at Todd, who was standing by himself near the picture window. He looked very much alone. And where was his girlfriend, Gin-Yung? Todd looked uncomfortable and out of place.

"Well—" Nick began.

"Nick Fox, what a surprise!" a syrupy voice interrupted him. A cloud of strong flowery perfume enveloped both him and Jessica as Celine slithered up to him. She was encased in a dark purple dress that was so tight, Jessica wondered how she avoided bursting the seams.

Nick smiled politely at her. "Hi, Celine."

Jessica instantly felt her back arch like an angry cat's. "Celine," she said sweetly. "What a *surprise* to see you here, since if I remember correctly, you weren't invited."

Celine simpered. "Oh, well, considering that *surprise* is the theme of this little party . . ." She giggled girlishly and put her hand on Nick's arm. "I just can't resist being part of all this"—Celine waved her other hand around the room—"happiness and high emotion." She lowered her lashes. "Do you blame me for tagging along with the other Thetas?"

Jessica stared daggers at Celine and restrained herself from pushing Celine away from Nick.

"Well, Jess did invite the entire sorority. So I guess that would include would-be Thetas too," he assured her, smiling and baring straight white teeth. "As long as you're in the right spirit of things, I don't think anyone will mind."

Jessica sputtered and shot him a killer look. *Traitor, how dare you cozy up to horrible Celine!*

"I hope you'll allow me to introduce you to my friends one of these days, Nick. They'd love to meet you, I'm sure," Celine said silkenly. She looked into Nick's eyes meaningfully.

"I thought the Thetas were your friends," Jessica couldn't resist saying.

"They're my *new* friends. I'm talking about my *old* friends." Celine squeezed Nick's arm and answered Jessica without taking her eyes from Nick's face. "These are people you wouldn't know, Jessica."

Jessica slid her arm through Nick's and pulled him away from Celine. "Nor would I *want* to. Nick has good taste, Celine." Jessica snuggled up against Nick. "He doesn't hang out with psychos." She smiled savagely at Celine.

Nick cleared his throat. "Not if I can help it. But I'd like to meet as many people at SVU as I can. You can never have too many friends, especially when you're new in town."

Celine's eyes glittered icily at Jessica; then she turned toward Nick. "Wonderful, it's a date," she crooned, her eyes now limpid pools. "We'll get together *soon*, I promise. But I have some business I must attend to." Celine threw him a gushing smile before disappearing into the crowd.

Jessica was stunned. She yanked her arm from Nick's. Nick had assured her that Celine wasn't his type, and now he was practically setting up a date with her right in front of Jessica.

Putting her hands on her hips, she faced him with

a fierce glare. "If you wanted to be with Celine, you shouldn't have come here with me."

"Jessica," he began calmly.

"Don't bother, Nick," Jessica said in a low voice. "I've had people lie to me before. I thought you said that Celine wasn't your type."

"She isn't, but can't I be nice to her? I feel sorry for her."

"Are you kidding?" Jessica's voice rose two octaves. "Celine is deranged," she snapped, her eyes stormy. "And you'd better be careful around her."

Nick caught Jessica's hand in his and met her eyes directly. "I don't want to date Celine, and that's the truth." Nick continued in a soft voice, "She just doesn't seem that terrible to me. Actually she looks pretty harmless."

Jessica sighed and let Nick hold her hand. "Just remember, Nick, looks can be deceiving."

Tom buried his face in his hands. He couldn't stand it. The thought of going out to dinner tonight and pretending everything was fine made him ill. His hangover had subsided, but his bad mood was getting worse.

Danny was out for the evening, and Tom was glad. He wanted to be by himself tonight.

Elizabeth would just have to understand. He thrust his hands through his hair and sighed deeply. They'd have to postpone the birthday dinner until another night.

Tom got up from his desk and sank down on his

bed. He grabbed his notebook and stared. He had worked hard on the family-tree project for his sociology class. For the past two hours he'd meticulously recorded his entire line of ancestors. It depressed him that he had no living relatives to write down.

Tom was the only one left.

He slowly ran his finger across the page, tracing the names of his parents, sister, and brother.

Closing the notebook, Tom flopped back on the bed. He was too tired to get up and turn off the lights.

This was one birthday he was going to skip.

Elizabeth took a deep breath. This was it. The party was going to happen in the next hour, and the worrying would finally be over. And it was about time. Between helping Mr. Conroy and trying to cheer a grumpy Tom, she was an absolute wreck!

Elizabeth ran nervous hands over the material of her new dress. The pale blue mandarin dress had cost more than she usually spent on clothes, but she wanted to look spectacular. She'd even had her hair professionally styled in loose waves down her back. Tonight was a very special night. *This is more than a surprise birthday party. This is my way of showing Tom how much he means to me,* Elizabeth thought seriously.

Elizabeth knocked on Tom's door, anxiously licking her lips. She put a happy smile on her face.

"Come in," came a sleepy voice.

Elizabeth's smile faded as she stared at Tom, who was sitting on his bed half dressed. In tan slacks that contrasted almost comically with his blue T-shirt and unshaven face, Tom looked anything but ready for a night on the town.

Tom met her eyes and threw her an apologetic look. "I'm sorry, Liz. I just don't feel up to celebrating tonight." He looked depressed as he nudged aside his dressy shoes. "I was going to pretend that I was happy and thrilled about my birthday, but I just can't go through with it."

Elizabeth sat down next to him, scooting a pile of papers over to one side. "Don't you think that getting out of this room might be good for you . . . that dressing up and eating a good meal might take your mind off your bad mood?" She reached for his hand.

Tom shook his head, his eyes shadowed with doubt. "I really don't know, Liz. I hate to let you down. . . ." His eyes finally registered Elizabeth's dressy appearance. "You look great, and you deserve an escort that looks and acts better than me." A shaky smile tugged at his lips.

Elizabeth studied his gloomy face for a second and slipped her arms around his waist. Hugging him hard, she took a light tone. "Are you really suggesting I go out scouting for a new boyfriend—at this late hour?" She met his eyes with a teasing smile.

Tom's face brightened reluctantly. If there was one thing Elizabeth had always appreciated, it was Tom's ability to laugh at himself. He put his arms around her and kissed her forehead. "No way. I may think you deserve a better man than me, but I'm much too selfish to make the sacrifice." His lips found hers in a short but intense kiss. "Can't we reschedule and do this another night?" he pleaded, stroking her hair gently.

No! Elizabeth thought in a frenzy. "We could, but I ordered an incredibly amazing dinner and had to pay up front since the restaurant had to special order it," Elizabeth said, suddenly inspired. "But if you really, really don't want to go—"

Tom scratched his stubbly jaw. "I don't know. . . ."

"I had the chef whip up your favorite dishes. He's using ingredients flown in from all over the world," Elizabeth intoned, her eyes round and pitiful.

Tom sighed and ran his hands through his hair. "OK, OK. I can't be an ogre and ruin everything." He got to his feet, grabbing a shirt and tie and his shaving kit. "I'll go get ready."

Elizabeth felt the tension ooze out of her body. She sank back onto the bed. "You won't be sorry. Tonight is going to be incredible, beyond your wildest dreams."

"I'll take your word for it," he murmured, stooping to pull out a pair of socks from his drawer.

Elizabeth held up a new binder that had been stacked on top of the pile of papers on his bed. "What's this?"

"My family-tree project for sociology. I was

proofreading it for the millionth time when you knocked." Tom rose and reached for the doorknob.

"If you want, I can check it for you again. Sometimes a fresh pair of eyes can be helpful."

"Thanks, Liz. That'll be great. I'll be back in a minute." Tom looked resigned, but at least he was smiling.

As the door softly shut behind him, Elizabeth opened the binder. She hoped creating a family tree hadn't been too painful for Tom. Writing down the names of the loved ones he'd lost could easily reinforce his sense of aloneness. This assignment couldn't have come at a worse time.

Idly her eyes scanned the names branching out across the page. Suddenly her eyes double backed, and she blinked. It couldn't be. But there it was. Clearly written in Tom's handwriting was his mother's full name, Joan Antoniani. Joan Antoniani! Elizabeth didn't know whether to laugh or cry. With a trembling finger she traced the name. It didn't make sense—Tom's father had died in a car crash. How could George Conroy . . .

"Is my family tree *that* fascinating?" Tom asked, sounding amused as he appeared in the doorway.

Elizabeth's heart leapt guiltily. She looked up with a pale face that was immediately suffused in red. "What? Oh yes, it is interesting—very." She closed the binder with a snap and gave Tom a wobbly smile. Tom was dressed, shaved, and ready to go.

Elizabeth didn't have time to tell him how good

he looked. Springing to her feet, she spun a quick story. "I forgot to tell Jess that her new boyfriend called. She'll kill me," she explained hurriedly. Tom was watching her so calmly that it was all she could do not to blurt out the truth. "I'll use the phone in the lobby. It was a long message, so it may take a while. I don't want to tie up your phone, since I'm sure all your friends will be calling to wish you a happy birthday." Elizabeth's smile felt phony and made her lips hurt.

Tom nodded amiably and settled back to look through some notes.

Pulse pounding in her throat, Elizabeth tore out of the room and down to the lobby. *Oh, Tom.* Her mind whirled crazily. *If this is true, it's an incredible miracle.* Tom wasn't an orphan anymore. He wasn't alone. Elizabeth crossed her fingers and prayed this would work out.

She dialed with sweating, shaking hands. "Mr. Conroy? You won't believe what I've found. . . ."

Chapter Eleven

Alex wanted to hide. "Oh no. What's Noah doing here?" she asked herself as Noah came right toward her. She squeezed her hands tightly together and tried to look nonchalant.

The party was overflowing with people, but she felt as if she stood out like a sore thumb. Alex was convinced that the green linen dress she was wearing was all wrong.

"Hi, Alex," Noah said casually. He looked devastatingly handsome and aloof. "I'm dying to try some of that punch." He pointed to the big serving bowl.

Alex's face burned. She had forgotten she was standing by the refreshment table. *I thought he was coming over to talk to me,* she thought, humiliated.

"Hope you're having a good time. I know I am," Noah commented as he ladled the bright red liquid into a glass. "Let's say we call a truce for the night.

You do your thing, and I'll do mine." He smiled coolly and nodded.

Tiffany Harkins called from across the room, "Hey, Noah. Over here! I haven't talked to you in ages." Her pretty face was eager as she motioned to Noah.

Alex forced a smile onto her paralyzed lips. "That's fine with me, Noah. I've got friends waiting for me, so I'll see you later," she lied. She tried not to watch as Noah hurried over to Tiffany, who threw her arms around him. Alex's stomach tightened as Noah let Tiffany drink from his glass.

"I've got to find someone to talk to," she muttered. "I don't want Noah thinking I'm a wallflower." She was glad the noise level was so high that no one could hear her talk to herself.

Frantically Alex searched the room for a friendly face. She felt ridiculous standing around by herself. Everyone else was in pairs or small groups. She grabbed a tumbler of orange soda, grateful to have something to hang on to. Thankfully she saw Isabella Ricci on the other side of the room. Relieved, Alex started to head toward her when she saw Lila Fowler stroll over to Isabella. Alex turned away. Two was company—three was a crowd. Especially when the third was Alexandra Rollins.

Alex swallowed back a lump in her throat. She couldn't help but watch as Noah stood close to Tiffany. Did he really *have* to put his arm around her?

"How's it going, Alex?" a familiar voice asked.

Alex jumped and choked violently on a mouthful of soda. Drops splattered down her forest green dress.

Todd Wilkins looked surprised. "Sorry, I didn't mean to scare you." He pounded on her back while she gasped for air.

Coughing and swabbing at her tearing eyes, Alex nodded. "That's OK," she croaked, waving her hand. "I'm fine." She grabbed a paper napkin from the refreshment table and dabbed at her dress. "How's it going, Todd?" She smiled shakily up at him with watery eyes.

Todd grabbed another napkin and handed it to her. "Maybe this is a sign I should just go home," he said with a sheepish smile. He glanced at the birthday banner with Tom's name on it. "I don't exactly fit in here."

Alex cleared her throat. She wanted to ask Todd to stay and talk with her, but she couldn't speak. Her throat was so irritated, she could only squeak.

Todd patted her shoulder. "Take care, Alex. Guess I'll go say hi to Danny."

Alex's heart sank even further. Spending time with Todd would have boosted her spirits. Todd was a friend, and during a time when they'd both been down and out, he'd been even more. She wished he'd stuck around.

"You look like you need some company!" a deep voice boomed.

Someone clapped Alex hard on the shoulder, making her splash her drink down her dress again. She whirled around in a fury.

"Look what you made me do!" she cried, wiping at her dress with her soggy napkin.

She glared at Jared Shepherd, who'd nearly knocked her off her feet. Kurt Albright was standing next to Jared, and both were grinning at Alex in a way that made her recoil. These two belonged to the Beta fraternity, which was a notch beneath even the Sigmas when it came to obnoxious behavior. Alex had a sinking sensation that she'd once met them at a party during her drinking days.

Jared leaned a heavy arm on Alex's shoulder, and she could smell the liquor on his breath. "Hey, babe, don't sweat it." He looked knowingly at her half-empty glass. "Looks like you just need a little refill." He flashed open his jacket and showed her a flask inside. Then he waved his own glass in front of her. He was drinking mostly booze with only a drop of punch.

Alex was immediately tense. "No, thanks, I'm only drinking soft drinks tonight," she said, trying to sound calm.

"Who are you trying to kid?" Jared laughed raucously. "She's a great kidder, isn't she, Kurt? We know all about you, Alex. You're a party girl. You know how to have fun, and soda pop is definitely not going to help." He and Kurt hooted and slapped each other's hands, swaying wildly. Alex realized the two were seriously intoxicated.

Kurt nudged his buddy. "Maybe she wants a sip straight from the bottle, man. She's not as picky as she looks." Chortling, he dumped most of the contents of his own glass of pure alcohol into Alex's glass.

The smell of whiskey made Alex want to retch, and the liquor slopped over her glass. She looked in dismay as it splattered her shoes. "Oh no," she wailed. "These shoes are suede."

Jared patted her roughly on the shoulder. "Well, drink up and you won't be worrying about your shoes."

"Unless," Kurt added brightly, "her shoes need a little drink too." He deliberately dribbled drops from his glass onto her shoes.

The two laughed and howled like insane hyenas, and Alex began feeling more than tense. Fear welled up inside as she stared at her glass full of liquor. Jared and Kurt pressed in closer, one on each side, until she felt like the very soggy, very scared filling in a loser sandwich. Her heart was hammering wildly and the room began to spin.

Jared pushed the glass up to Alex's lips. "Open wide, it's time for your drinky!"

Alex shut her eyes. She could almost taste the whiskey and found she didn't have the will to pull away.

Kurt grabbed Alex's jaw as if to squeeze her mouth open and said, "Maybe she wants you to feed it to her."

"And maybe she doesn't," a husky voice asserted coolly.

Alex's eyes flew open, and she gaped in shock. It was Nick Fox, Jessica's new boyfriend. He was suddenly standing in front of Kurt and Jared.

"What did you say, pretty boy?" Jared looked outraged and took a menacing step forward, swelling up his chest.

Nick reached forward and smoothly pulled Alex from their grasp. He took the glass from her nerveless fingers and set it on the punch table. He stepped in front of Alex. "The lady doesn't want to drink with you gentlemen. Why don't you take your little party somewhere else?" His tone was bland, but Alex felt herself begin to quake with nerves. The look on Nick's face was scarier than anything she'd ever seen before.

Jared and Kurt were too drunk to notice. Jared crumpled his cup and dropped the mess to the floor. Red faced, he began flexing his arm muscles.

Kurt pushed his face into Nick's. "What'sa matter with you, boy—you some kind of prissy little mama's boy? You some kind of weirdo out to stop us from having a little fun?" He grabbed Nick's arm while Jared bodychecked him roughly. Alex could see they were trying to knock Nick off his feet. "You mind your own business or I'm gonna kick your butt," Kurt snarled.

"I don't think so," Nick said, his voice soft and deadly. In a flash Nick locked an arm around Kurt's throat and twisted his right wrist behind his back. Kurt's face turned a sickly ashen gray as he squirmed helplessly in Nick's grip. "If you make a move," Nick warned through his teeth to Jared. His voice was so low, Alex barely heard it. "I'll have to hurt your buddy here."

Jared looked uncertain but hostile. "Oh yeah, like I'm scared," he said in a swaggering voice. His eyes were darting uneasily.

Alex gaped in amazement. Nick fought like a pro. She'd only seen people move like that on TV.

Nick shrugged and stared unflinchingly at Kurt. "Looks like your friend doesn't care what happens to you."

"He means it, man," Kurt whimpered. "Back off, Jared. The guy's a wacko."

Jared stepped clumsily backward.

Nick still didn't loosen his hold. "You two can go quietly out that door on your own." He nodded toward the exit. "Or you can go out on stretchers. Your choice."

Jared and Kurt bobbed their heads up and down quickly, their eyes shifting eagerly toward escape. Nick released Kurt but didn't drop his vigilant stance. Alex could see that if either of the two made a wrong move, Nick wouldn't hesitate to pounce.

Jared and Kurt wasted no time as they barreled through the crowd, speeding up as they reached the exit. Muttering curses and throwing vicious looks over their shoulders at Nick, they were soon out the door.

Alex went limp with relief. Her thundering heart was slowing down, and she tightly interlaced her hands to stop them from shaking. The front of her green dress had dark spots all over it and her shoes were ruined, but she felt enormously better.

"Thanks," she whispered hoarsely to Nick, who was cleaning up the mess on the floor with a wad of napkins.

He glanced up at her. "No problem. I hate bullies, especially ones who try to force something on someone who clearly doesn't want it." Nick rose easily, dumping the napkins into a trash can.

Alex smiled at him uncertainly, grateful that he'd gotten rid of the creeps. But there was something she had to ask. She stepped closer to him and looked over her shoulder, feeling a little silly. "So, Nick . . . where did you learn to fight like that? I've only seen those moves on real-life cop programs." Alex's voice died to a whisper.

Nick's green eyes were hard as glass for a second. Nick studied her until Alex began to squirm a bit. Finally he took a deep breath and seemed to make a decision. "Listen, Alex, what I'm about to tell you is for your ears only—got it? And the only reason I'm telling you is because I can't have you telling anyone what you just saw me do. You can't tell anyone else." He smiled reassuringly at her. "Not even your boyfriend."

Alex nodded, completely in the dark. *You mean ex-boyfriend,* a miserable voice in her head mocked. "But what about those two guys?"

Nick leaned closer to her and lowered his voice. "Those losers are too drunk to remember their names. Listen, Alex, I'm an undercover narc. But no one can know about it. If anyone finds out, I could be in serious danger. It could even mean my life." His expression was serious and intent, and Alex felt as if the wind had been knocked out of her. Nick Fox was a cop.

"Does Jessica know?" Alex asked with sudden interest.

He shook his head. "No, and she can't find out. I'm counting on you and trusting you, Alex." He smiled ruefully at her. "You could say my life depends on you keeping your promise."

Alex was earnest. "I won't tell a soul. I promise. Not Jessica, not Noah, not anyone." She put her hand shyly on his. "You can trust me."

Nick looked relieved. "I hate burdening you with my secret, but in a way I'm glad you know. Because maybe now I can help you." His warm, velvety voice made Alex feel good and safe.

"Help me?"

Nick quietly handed her a card. It read: SVU Drug and Alcohol Abuse Hotline. It stated that it offered referrals, support, and information.

Alex felt her face flame up, and she couldn't meet Nick's eyes as she asked softly, "How did you know?"

"It was nothing obvious, but a buddy of mine has been fighting an addiction for years. You get to know the signs." Nick's expression was gentle and nonjudgmental.

Alex tucked the card into her purse and looked Nick bravely in the eye. "I'm going to give them a call. And I'll keep your secret, Nick. I promise." Her smile was fragile.

Nick nodded. "I know you will, Alex. I trust you."

Chapter Twelve
_____

Tom tried not to sigh too loudly. Elizabeth was so pleased with herself and so happy as she led him up the steps of La Casa Blanca restaurant that he couldn't bear to burst her bubble. The moonlight turned her hair into pure silver and highlighted her flawless face.

"You look gorgeous, Liz. Too good for me, that's for sure," Tom said in a self-mocking tone.

"Oh, you." Elizabeth pushed him teasingly. She dimpled up at him, and he forced himself to smile broadly back at her.

La Casa Blanca was a new Mexican restaurant. Normally Tom would have been psyched for the experience, ready to sink his teeth into his favorite dishes, but tonight he wasn't in the mood. *I can't let Liz down, though,* he reminded himself. *I've been such an ogre lately, and it's not her fault.* Tom was feeling better than he had that morning. His hangover had finally dissipated.

"I hope you've worked up an appetite," Elizabeth chattered, her eyes sparkling. "I ordered the yummiest dishes for us tonight."

Tom smiled slightly. They had just entered the restaurant and the aromas were inviting. "It's hard not to be hungry when you're bombarded with such delicious shrimp and fajita smells."

Elizabeth led him right past the maître d' and through the tables.

He halted. "Hey, shouldn't we give our name or something? Shouldn't we wait to be seated?"

Elizabeth shook her head. "Nope, I've reserved a private table in the back." She looked up at him, her sea-colored eyes like stars. "I promise this will be special. Our table is in here." She pointed to a door with the name Blue Room embossed in gold above it.

Tom opened the door and blinked. A roomful of people were shouting and singing. Confetti rained down on his head. Someone was tooting "Happy Birthday" on a kazoo. Balloons and streamers floated overhead. Cameras flashed. People yelled, "Surprise!" as they clapped and stomped their feet on the floor.

Tom turned to Elizabeth, who had tears glowing in her eyes. "Happy birthday," she cried joyfully, throwing her arms around him.

Tom looked around the room, which was bursting with what seemed to be hundreds of people. There was Danny grinning at him. Winston Egbert was playing "For He's a Jolly Good Fellow" on the kazoo. Isabella Ricci was singing along. He recognized the faces from WSVU as they flung glittering confetti at him.

Tom grabbed Elizabeth and kissed her, swirling her off her feet. There was thunderous applause and a few voices chanted, "Speech, speech!" He gently set her down but held her close beside him.

Tom laughed and shook his head, mouthing, "No speech for now." This was the most amazing thing he'd ever experienced. Overwhelmed by the warmth and love in the room, he felt a tingling of tears in his own eyes. He'd never realized how much his friends cared about him.

Elizabeth slipped her hand into his. "I'm glad you like it, Tom. I was so afraid you might be mad." She leaned her head against his shoulder. "I was so busy with your party all week. That's why I wasn't around much."

Tom squeezed her hand. "I really appreciate this, Liz. I feel like a jerk, getting upset with you when you were planning all of this for me." He reached down to kiss her again.

She laughed happily, cheeks flushed with excitement. "Don't worry about it. All that matters is that you have a good time. After all, you're the guest of honor," Elizabeth reassured him. "By the way, Danny, Bryan, Nina, and Winston helped put this together too. I don't want to take all the credit."

"I'll have to thank everybody. I can't believe you guys were able to keep the party a secret."

"Boy, it wasn't easy. You're not the best journalist

around for nothing. There were a few times when I thought you might have figured it out." Elizabeth smiled affectionately at him and reached up to pat his cheek.

"You're telling me," Danny chimed in. He came up beside them and smacked Tom affectionately on the arm. "You're a hard man to keep a secret from. I kept thinking those eagle eyes of yours were going to blow our cover."

Tom clapped him on the back and grinned at his friend. "You guys were too good. Thanks, man. I really appreciate all this."

Isabella, who was right behind Danny, reached up to hug Tom and kiss his cheek. She quickly fastened a silvery, sequined, cone-shaped party hat on top of his head.

"Hey, no fair." Tom threw up his hands and tried to pull off the hat.

"You have to wear the hat at least until you cut the cake—that's the law," Nina teased as she ran up to give Tom a big hug.

"Nina!" Elizabeth looked at her friend with wide eyes. "Your hair—I love it. You look absolutely gorgeous!"

"Absolutely gorgeous," Isabella echoed.

"It's unanimous." Danny nodded.

"Thanks for helping with my party, Nina," Tom said, returning Nina's hug. Nina did look great. Tom had always thought she was an attractive girl, but now, with the braids gone, replaced by a shorter hairstyle, she looked stunning. Soft curls framed her face and danced around her collarbone. "You look really good. I like the hair." He smiled into Nina's beaming eyes. "Where's the Bry-man?" he asked, searching the crowd for Bryan. "I want to thank him too."

"He's getting everyone who hasn't signed your card yet to sign it now," Nina said. She rolled her eyes but smiled. "You know Bryan, organized down to the last second."

Tom waved to Winston and Denise. He grinned as they both blew kisses to him. He saw several faces he recognized and a few he didn't. "There are so many people here. I can't believe it."

"Well, there's a reason for that. Jessica invited a 'few' of her friends," Nina put in wryly, her eyes meeting Elizabeth's.

Elizabeth shrugged helplessly.

Tom chuckled knowingly. "Speaking of which, where is the other Ms. Wakefield?"

"She's around somewhere. Knowing Jess, she's probably already cooking up some new 'surprise.'" Elizabeth made a mock grimace. "We'll just have to wait and see."

"I should warn you guys," Nina said in a lowered voice. She looked quickly left and right. "Somehow Celine found out about the party. I don't see her now, but I know she's lurking around."

Elizabeth gasped and turned white. "*What!* You've got to be kidding!"

Nina shook her head. "Sorry, I wish I were."

Elizabeth stared at Tom. "I can't believe it. When did she crawl out of her hole? I thought we were free of Celine forever."

"I don't know the story. Rumor has it that your sister does, though," Nina said.

"That figures."

"I doubt Jessica invited her," Nina said soothingly. "I'm pretty sure Celine crashed this shindig."

Tom caressed Elizabeth's shoulder. "It doesn't matter. Even Celine can't ruin this night. Nobody can. Let's just pretend she's a mirage."

"If only it were that simple," muttered Elizabeth.

"Anyway, we're not going to let anyone or anything spoil old Tombo's party," Danny interjected. "Even if the guest of honor looks pretty silly in his party hat." Danny adjusted the hat so that it cocked over one of Tom's eyebrows.

"Cute," Tom said as he pushed the hat back. "Can I take this off now?"

"Nope," Isabella answered pertly. "You heard Nina—not until you cut your cake."

"You mean I have to sit through dinner like this. . . ."

Elizabeth giggled at Tom's expression. "I think he looks adorable." She hugged his waist.

Before Tom could respond, another voice joined the fray. "Hey, Watts," a bass voice boomed. Matt Wylie strode up and slapped Tom's open palm. "Way to go! Happy birthday!" Matt was an old friend and a football player. He and Tom had played together before Tom quit. Tom was surprised and happy to see him. How did Elizabeth track down so many people from his past?

Tom introduced Matt to Liz, and as he shook hands with everyone Tom whispered to Elizabeth, "You know, Liz, I've been feeling low about not having my family with me anymore, but right now I feel pretty lucky. How can I be depressed when I have so many friends?" He felt a lump in his throat as he smiled deeply into her eyes. "You couldn't have given me a better birthday present."

Elizabeth's eyes shone softly. "Just wait," she said tenderly. "You haven't even seen my gift yet."

"I can't see. I can't see. Does he look surprised? What's going on?" Jessica craned her neck but couldn't spot Tom and Elizabeth over the sea of people.

"Everything's going as planned. Tom's laughing and kissing your sister," Nick assured her. He easily towered over the crowd.

Laughter and conversation from the revelers rose to an intense buzzing level. The music was blaring across the room, and Jessica had to nearly shout to get Nick's attention.

"I said my throat is dry and I'm dying for a drink!"

He frowned in puzzlement. "You have to think? What do you have to think about?"

"No, not think—drink!" Jessica broke into giggles.

She stood on tiptoe and spoke directly into his ear. "I'm thirsty—I need something to drink."

Nick grinned. "OK, I got it. Why don't I go get us something? Diet cola with lots of ice, right?"

"Yes—please hurry. I'm dying." Jessica draped a dramatic hand across her forehead.

"I don't blame you. I'm burning up in here myself." Nick looked amused at her theatrics and tugged off his jacket. "Would you hold this while I squeeze my way through the crowd?"

Jessica nodded and gathered the jacket into her arms. The gray material was very soft and it smelled great, like Nick. The party had been a blast so far, and everything was going as smooth as silk, despite snaky Celine trying to sink her fangs into Nick. The only odd moment was when she saw Nick deep in conversation with Alexandra Rollins. Nick had told her he'd helped Alex get rid of some drunken creeps who'd been bothering her. Jessica hadn't minded his heroics. Actually, she was proud of him.

Jessica sighed and adjusted her arms under Nick's jacket. The room was getting very warm, and even though the back of her slinky black mini was cut out, she was feeling hot and flushed. Jessica wished Nick would hurry back, and she tried to search the throngs of people for a glimpse of him. Jessica was so thirsty, she was about to walk over and grab the glass of punch from Kimberly Schyler's hand.

Jessica was distracted from her fantasies by a glimpse of golden hair that looked exactly like her own. Except the golden hair was above a prim, high-necked blue dress that Jessica would never have worn in a million years. It was her twin, and Elizabeth was talking to Winston, smiling and pointing. Tom stood behind her, nodding at something Danny was saying. Jessica supposed she would eventually have to make her way over to Tom and wish him a happy birthday.

The music was stopped abruptly as Winston talked into the microphone. "Attention, fellow partyers. Elizabeth has asked me to tell you that the buffet will be ready in about fifteen minutes. So you chowhounds should get your forks ready!"

Some people started cheering, while others drifted over to the buffet table. Winston bowed and turned the CD player back on.

Jessica didn't blame people for lining up for food; she was starting to get hungry herself. She craned her neck, but Elizabeth and Tom were no longer in sight. Without warning a soft *brrrring* exploded under her arm.

Jessica jumped. There it was again. Jessica could feel Nick's jacket vibrating. It was his phone! Nick's cellular phone was ringing. Should she answer it? This could be the chance she was waiting for. She'd been racking her brains, trying to figure out Nick's secrets, and the solution was suddenly right in her hands.

She answered it quickly and grunted as deeply as possible, "Yeah?" Jessica hoped she'd sufficiently disguised her voice.

A man answered quickly, "Yeah. The package will be ready for pickup at two A.M. tonight. Behind the science building. That's tonight, two A.M., science building," he repeated in shorthand.

"Uh," Jessica said in a gruff voice, hoping the guy would take her mumbling as a yes. She listened to the click on the other end. He had hung up.

Jessica stared at the phone. Hands slick with sweat and shaking violently, she shoved the phone back into Nick's coat.

Nick reached her side seconds later, and Jessica nearly screamed. That was a close one. Nick grinned at her and handed her a drink. "Here you go, wild child. Diet cola on ice, just the way you like it." He took a sip of his own soda.

"Thanks," Jessica squeaked. She cleared her throat. "I mean . . . thanks, Nick. You're sweet." She gazed at him through long lashes and took a long gulp of soda. She really needed it! Jessica's pulse had finally slowed down when she noticed Nick watching her with a funny expression on his face.

"I think I was severely dehydrated," she improvised swiftly. She licked her lips and gave him a charming smile.

"I'm so glad I revived you," Nick said into her ear. "I definitely want you alive and well." He brushed his lips softly against hers. Jessica felt herself shiver with delight as she pressed her lips enthusiastically against his. They came up for air and gazed at each other for a heartbeat.

"Nice party," Nick said casually. He took his jacket from her hands, a sexy smile curving his lips. "What do you think, Jess?" He reached to caress her cheek.

"This evening has been outstanding," Jessica agreed. And what Nick didn't know was that tonight was going to be even more memorable than he imagined. Jessica would finally uncover all his secrets. *I'm going to that meeting at two A.M., and I'll find out what you're up to.*

"Where is he?" Elizabeth muttered under her breath. "I'll just die if he doesn't show up. . . ." Elizabeth felt her stomach rumble with nerves and hunger. She snuck a discreet peek at her watch. Thank heavens, they'd be setting up the food any minute. She glanced anxiously at the door.

It's still a little early, she reassured herself. Tom and Danny were arguing in good humor about which peppers were the hottest, but she was barely following their conversation. *What if he gets lost?* Elizabeth was jolted out of her thoughts when Tom gently nudged her. "What do you think, Liz? Is it better to eat hot peppers whole or chopped up in tiny pieces?" He was dangling on one finger the party hat Isabella had given him.

Elizabeth winced. "I try and eat peppers as sparingly as possible."

Danny smiled broadly at her. "You haven't lived until you've downed a whole Thai pepper in one gulp."

Tom punched his arm affectionately. "I've got to

see you pull that off, Wyatt. I'll be standing by with a fire extinguisher."

Danny chuckled loudly. "Great, we'll have a pepper-eating contest. You name the place and date."

Elizabeth froze; her heart shot upward. There he was. Mr. Conroy had just entered the room.

"Will you be our witness, Liz?" Tom had his arm around her shoulders, a teasing gleam in his eyes. He looked so happy and relaxed.

Elizabeth stammered for a moment, aware that Tom and Danny were watching her. She answered quickly. "Sure, uh . . . I'll be your witness. Tom, I—um, hate to interrupt, but there's something—er—some surprise I want to show you." Elizabeth turned toward Danny. "Do you mind if I steal him away for a minute? I have something private planned for him."

"This doesn't involve a scantily clad woman jumping out of a cake, does it?" Tom laughed as he leaned down to kiss Elizabeth's cheek.

Danny joined in heartily and reached over to ruffle Tom's hair. "In your dreams, Tombo. He's all yours, Elizabeth." Danny rubbed his stomach playfully and grabbed Tom's party hat, slapping it onto his own head. "I'm on my way to the buffet line. This man is hungry and ready to eat. Maybe your hat will get me to the front of the line." He grinned, threw them a pretend salute, and disappeared into the crowd.

"So what's the big secret, Liz?" Tom mused.

Elizabeth tugged him toward the other end of the room. "You'll see," she answered weakly. Mr. Conroy was standing in the corner, looking nervous and eager. A few partygoers seemed to notice him. Elizabeth watched them look at him curiously. She could tell they were trying to figure out what a well-dressed, middle-aged man was doing at a party full of college kids.

"This way, Tom," she murmured, trying not to drag him too forcefully.

I hope I'm doing the right thing, she thought with a racing heart. *I just want to make these two people happy.*

Mr. Conroy was only a few feet away. Well, it was too late. There was no turning back.

Elizabeth caught a glimpse of Tom's puzzled face as she brought him to Mr. Conroy's side. She released Tom's hand, and he stood as still as a statue. Mr. Conroy's brown eyes were fastened on Tom, shining with intense emotion. Elizabeth thought Mr. Conroy looked as if he might collapse.

Here goes nothing.

Elizabeth said a quick prayer, cleared her throat, and slipped her arm through Mr. Conroy's. "Tom, I wanted this birthday to be your best ever. What I didn't realize at first was that I could make your wildest dreams come true. I know you've been longing to have a family again." She raised her eyes to meet Tom's confused ones. Elizabeth sent him a gentle, comforting smile.

Tom shook his head, dazed. "I don't know what you're talking about, Liz."

"This will definitely be a shock to you," Elizabeth said in a soft voice. Mr. Conroy's arm was trembling under her hand.

"What's going on?" Tom whispered.

"Tom, I'd like you to meet your father—George Conroy."

The *valley* has never been so *sweet*!

Having left Sweet Valley High School behind them, Jessica and Elizabeth Wakefield have begun a new stage in their lives, attending the most popular university around – Sweet Valley University!

Join them and all their friends for fun, frolics and frights on *and* off campus.

Ask your bookseller for any titles you may have missed. The Sweet Valley University series is published by Bantam Books.

We hope you enjoyed reading this book. If you would like to receive further information about available titles in the Bantam series, just write to the address below, with your name and address:

KIM PRIOR
Bantam Books
61–63 Uxbridge Road
London W5 5SA

If you live in Australia or New Zealand and would like more information about the series, please write to:

SALLY PORTER
Transworld Publishers (Australia) Pty Ltd
15–25 Helles Avenue
Moorebank
NSW 2170
AUSTRALIA

KIRI MARTIN
Transworld Publishers (NZ) Ltd
3 William Pickering Drive
Albany
Auckland
NEW ZEALAND

All Transworld titles are available by post from:
Bookservice by Post, PO Box 29
Douglas, Isle of Man, IM99 1BQ

Credit Cards accepted.
Please telephone 01624 675137 or fax 01624 670923
or Internet http://www.bookpost.co.uk
or e-mail: bookshop@enterprise.net for details.

Free postage and packing in the UK.
Overseas customers allow £1 per book (paperbacks)
and £3 per book (hardbacks)